Carlo Gregorio Rosignoli

Choice of a State of Life

Carlo Gregorio Rosignoli

Choice of a State of Life

ISBN/EAN: 9783337428297

Printed in Europe, USA, Canada, Australia, Japan

Cover: Foto ©Andreas Hilbeck / pixelio.de

More available books at **www.hansebooks.com**

CHOICE

OF

A STATE OF LIFE.

BY FATHER C. G. ROSSIGNOLI, S. J.

Translated from the French.

PUBLISHED WITH THE APPROBATION OF
THE MOST REV. THE ARCHBISHOP OF BALTIMORE.

BALTIMORE:

PUBLISHED BY JOHN MURPHY & CO.

182 BALTIMORE STREET.

1868.

RE-IMPRIMATUR,

MARTIN JOHN,

Archbishop of Baltimore.

January, 1868.

iv

UNDER THE AUSPICES OF

The Blessed Virgin Mary,

THIS LITTLE WORK

IS HUMBLY DEDICATED TO

Catholic Youth.

THE translator has felt the need of a work like this, to guide him in choosing a State of Life; and his affection for you has induced him to publish what, at first, was intended only for those young friends by whom he is surrounded. Accept it, then, as a tribute of affection from a friend, who, being one of your number, has your spiritual welfare at heart: and should it guide even one of you to the state of life to which God invites him, he is content, and well rewarded for his labor.

CONTENTS.

PART I.

OF A WISE CHOICE IN GENERAL.

PART II.

OF A WISE CHOICE IN PARTICULAR.

INTRODUCTION.

I HAVE been induced, my dear Reader, to prepare this little work on the *Choice of a State of Life,* by an earnest desire to give you a faithful guide through the darkness that surrounds you in this world. And this desire is the more ardent, because those that choose well are often led to heaven, whilst such as make a bad choice, are generally lost for all eternity.

For a time I hesitated to present you with this little volume, lest you might imagine that I wished to draw you to the religious state. But the extreme need in which young persons stand of help and advice, and their inclination to decide without reflection, have caused me to disregard that objection: and I declare, my dear child, that it is the same to me, whether you become a religious, or lead a life in the world. My only desire is, that you should lead a holy life, and die a happy death. Since, however, it is impossible to do this unless you embrace the state of life to which God calls you, I beg you to listen to whatever He may whisper to your heart. Perhaps he calls you to some office or profession, which suits your inclination. If you find it so, obey with joy the heavenly call; for even courts and battle-fields have alike produced saints.

What does the Eternal Wisdom wish to teach us by the vision of Ezechiel, in which four mysterious animals draw the chariot of the divine glory? A man drawing beside a lion; an ox yoked with an eagle! What a strange combination! However, these four animals equally serve God. See the mystery; it is this: people of the world by their piety, and religious by faithfully practising Christian perfection, — merchants by their labors, and sages by their studies, — all contribute to the glory of God. Hear St. Augustine on this point: "The humble and the exalted come, the poor and the rich, the learned and the unlearned." Yes, heaven is open, not only to those who forsake the world, to the poor and the ignorant, but also to the rich and the learned, to princes, magistrates, and courtiers, — soldiers open the gates of heaven with the sword, bankers with gold.

Behold, on Mount Tabor, at the Transfiguration of Jesus, two persons very different, yet
equally renowned and glorious; one Moses, the
other Elias; Moses a courtier, Elias a hermit;
Moses as gentle, as meek as a lamb, Elias rough
and repulsive; Moses married and living amid
luxury, Elias single and worn down by fasting;
Moses wealthy and clad in rich robes, Elias poor
and covered with a hair shirt; Moses is of a disposition so kind, that through love for his people,
he causes water to gush from a rock, whilst Elias
shows a threatening zeal, and to frighten a nation,
hinders the clouds from sending down their show-
ers. However, in states of life so different, and
with conduct so opposite, these two men lived
according to God's heart, enjoyed the same glory,
and had the same privilege of assisting at the
Transfiguration of Jesus; and the Evangelist
does not even say, which was on the right, and
which on the left.

Perhaps it may be thought that I am showing
the inutility of my undertaking, because I pretend that the gates of heaven are open to all
states of life. It is not true, however, that all
roads, without distinction, conduct the pilgrim
thither; but it is generally very true, that those

do not reach heaven who wander from the path to which God has assigned them. St. Augustine and St. Ambrose remark that, of the four animals that drew the divine chariot, not one made a single step according to his own pleasure, but only as he was directed by the Holy Ghost. Moses and Elias by different roads reached the same glory; but observe, each quickly entered the way into which God called him: when they received the least sign, they replied in these admirable words: "Here I am." (Ex. iii. 4.) They generously placed themselves in his hands, that he might do with them whatever he pleased. If therefore, God calls you into the world, go without any uneasiness. But if he distinctly calls you to religion, why shut your eyes to this kind light, and run the risk of devoting them afterwards to eternal tears? I have no other object in view, than to hinder you from acting at hazard in this most important affair; so that, having weighed well all the reasons on either side, you can say with confidence: "I will enter this profession, because God desires me to do so; I will become a priest, because it is my vocation; I will join a religious order, because the Holy Ghost urges me in that direction; I will betake

myself to commerce, because God has given me
to understand that the riches of the world will
not make me lose eternal riches." My desire is,
to assist you in finding out the state to which God
calls you, and I am very far from endeavoring
by an indiscreet zeal to drag you into a cloister.
I may present you with some reasons, which
would seem to call you to a religious life, but
only through necessity; because it is at once the
most perfect state, and has the greatest number
of difficulties. Young persons, therefore, have
great need of help, that they may conquer them.
But there will be this advantage; those who feel
themselves led thither by the Holy Ghost, will
be encouraged in their undertaking; whilst those
who do not feel themselves thus called, and do
not think these same motives sufficient to determine them to a religious life, will act wisely in
avoiding it, and will live in peace, because they
will not have shut their hearts against Divine
inspirations. Thus, my work will be useful to
both. Read then with attention, and be perfectly
indifferent to all states of life. If you have a
fancy for any particular state, remove it, and
listen to the voice of God. When you hear this
voice, say with Moses, "Lord, here I am," do with

me as you please. Call me hither or thither; to the world, or to the cloister, and I obey the call.

Do not seek novelty in this little work, nor elegance of thought; I am content to write, with the greatest simplicity possible, the sentiments of the holy doctors, philosophers, and pious authors; sentiments, scattered through many volumes, upon the manner of choosing a state of life. If pearls could be gathered from a little stream they would enrich many men; but, being buried in vast seas, very few find them. I hope it will not be so with this collection of truths; though small, it will furnish an abundance of precious treasures to youth.

ON THE

CHOICE OF A STATE OF LIFE.

PART FIRST.

OF A WISE CHOICE IN GENERAL.

CHAPTER I.

SECTION 1. *To make a wise choice of a state of life, you must first know the end for which you are created.*

DIOGENES Laertius tells us, that Xenophon, from his earliest youth, was endowed with a disposition so amiable, and a mind so sublime, that he seemed rather heavenly than human. But there being no one to direct and instruct him, his precious talents were hidden, and all his views were limited to the desire of amassing wealth as a merchant, or of acquiring fame by the noble profession of arms. Socrates once met him, and perceiving in his countenance the marks of a great soul, stopped him and asked: "Whither are you going?"

Xenophon was much surprised and knew not what to reply. Socrates then asked: "Where do they sell the necessaries of life?" "At the market," replied the youth. "But," added the philosopher, "where do they sell those things that are necessary for living well?" Xenophon, much embarrassed, replied: "I know nothing about that." "Come," said Socrates, "I will show you." He took him by the hand, led him to his school, and developed in him those talents which posterity will never cease to admire.

Dear young friends, who have received from God, a soul — priceless, on account of its excellent dispositions, "Whither are you going?" Whither do your desires tend? What state of life will you embrace, in order to employ your talents? Ah! how many are there among you who remain silent, or bashfully reply: "I do not know." I hope there is none, who, abandoned to a brutal passion, will reply in the words of a certain youth, cited by Lucian. This reckless lad, mounted on a wild and unmanageable horse, hardly less reasonable than his rider, gave him the reins, and allowed himself to be borne into the midst of frightful precipices. A passer-by called out to him, "Whither are you going?" He replied,—

"Whithersoever this beast wishes to carry me."

Why then so much negligence in seeking the road to virtue and glory, and so much ardor in the pursuit of sensual pleasure and riches? Why refuse to be governed by reason, when you so easily yield to the fury of passion? Ah! allow yourself to be taken by the hand, and led to the school of true wisdom, there to learn the manner of choosing that state of life which corresponds to your talents, and to the graces you have received from Almighty God. To choose well, says St. Augustine, is to decide according to the light of reason, and especially of faith, in what state of life we can best secure the end for which we are created. We must, therefore, first learn what this end is, for which the Uncreated Wisdom has placed us in this world. Is it to become great men; celebrated scholars; wise magistrates; wealthy merchants, and nothing more? Natural reason and divine faith loudly proclaim, that He had quite another end in view. A mortal object cannot be the end of an immortal soul; and it can never constitute the happiness of a creature that bears the image of its Creator stamped on its mind. We must therefore say, that God created the world for the use of man, but made man to serve Him in this life, and to share His happiness in the life to come.

Behold then all that man is to do in this world; to merit the happiness of heaven, that he may pass from this short life of afflictions, to an eternal life of bliss. Oh! what a noble destiny! This glory was not your due; but God, through his infinite mercy, has created you to enjoy it. He could have created you for no other than natural happiness; but he has been pleased to destine you to a happiness that is supernatural. He has made other creatures for you, but has created you for himself alone.

No other creature has a nobler end; not even the angels, archangels, cherubim and seraphim, who are like yourself in having been created to enjoy eternal felicity in God.

This infallible truth presents two evident consequences; one, that the present life and its different states are but the means for obtaining our end — eternal happiness; the other, that the means are good and estimable, only so far as they assist us in attaining this end: temporal objects and the various states of life are good, only so far as they help us to gain eternal happiness by serving God. St. Ignatius established this first truth as the foundation of a good choice. These are his remarkable words: *"Man is created to praise and honor the Lord his God, and by serving him to save himself. All creatures on earth have been created on account of*

man, *to assist him in obtaining the end of his
creation. It therefore follows, that we ought to
use them or abstain from their use, only inas-
much as they do really lead us to our end, or
turn us from it.*"

SECTION 2. *The end of our creation should be
the first rule of a choice.*

EVERY thing in nature tends to its end by the
straightest path. We see it in the tendency of
heavy bodies towards the centre of the earth.
We too should choose that state which seems to
conduct us most directly and most surely to our
end, which is to serve God and afterwards enjoy
him, to tend towards him incessantly with all
the powers of our soul, with all the affections
of our heart.

If a stone, on its way towards the centre of
attraction, falls into water or fire, or is broken in
pieces, it matters but little, because its tendency
is still the same: provided, therefore, we obtain
our end, it matters little whether it be by a path
easy and strewn with flowers, or by one painful
and bristling with thorns. We are travellers on
earth ; and when a traveller has decided upon
the place he wishes to reach, if he finds many
tracks to the right and to the left, he follows
only the one that leads to his destination, and
troubles himself but little if it turns this way or

that, if it rises or descends, or is more or less
agreeable than others; easy or difficult, it is the
only road for him. Behold then, how we should
choose a state of life: we should seek only that
state which leads us to our end, and avoid those
that may draw us from it. If the ecclesiastical
state conducts you best to your end, hasten to
enter it. If riches and greatness lead you away
from it, shrink from them as you would from
poison. If the bar insures your cause for the
last judgment, this is the state that suits you
best. If mercantile pursuits endanger your
salvation, your real interest calls upon you to
give them up. If you find more assistance for
obtaining the end for which God has created
you, in a cell than in a palace, in hatred of the
world than in its slavery, in the sweet yoke of
Jesus than in gratifying your own will, you will
act wisely in choosing the way wherein the safer
means are found. In a word, it is always an
imprudence and a folly, to select a state without
having perfectly foreseen how you will obtain
your last end therein. Your choice can be wise,
only so far as it facilitates your salvation. Let
us conclude with the words of St. Augustine:
" He is the best off who has his way and walks
well therein." The only good state is that
which sets us forward on our way, and in which
we employ present time to acquire a happy
eternity.

It is then a great error, if, in contempt of this truth, you permit chance, or worldly interest, or the heat of imagination, to determine your choice. You then act blindly, forget the future, and think only of the present; you yield to caprice, and enter a road which may lead to precipices, and in which you have not always the possibility of turning back. I am deeply afflicted when I see souls, capable of great enterprises, shamefully pursuing contemptible objects, because they thoughtlessly embraced a state of life without knowing how to discover the good route. Unfortunate youths! they have gone astray at the first step without perceiving it. Now they are involved, without knowing how or why, in very dangerous affairs, and have no hope of ever getting rid of them. Had they chosen wisely at first, they would now be happy, and God would have revived in them a Charles Borromeo and a Leopold of Austria; whilst, on the contrary, we behold them in the world prostituting their talents to the vilest undertakings.

In order to preserve you from these misfortunes, I call upon you to pause in the beginning of your career, and hear the words of Cicero: *In primis constituendum est, quos nos, et quales esse velimus, et in quo genere vitæ;* before advancing in age and plunging into business, see what character you ought to act on the theatre of this world. You have many roads before you : you must follow one of them, and in order to decide which, consider beforehand whither these roads lead, and which will take you most directly to your destination. " *Choose the way before you run,*" says St. Ambrose : consider rather the end than the route. If you desire a way that presents pleasures, amusements and ornaments; a way beautifully paved (Eccl. xxi. 11,) take care that it leads not to darkness and suffering. If you fear to enter the road of virtue because it is narrow and difficult, be encouraged by the happy life to which it brings you.

CHAPTER II.

SECTION 1. *The choice of a state is the most important of all affairs.*

LOUIS of Grenada speaks like a wise and prudent man, (as he really was,) when he called the choice of a state, *the master-wheel* of the whole life: for if in a clock we remove the principal wheel, all the other wheels are stopped, and the clock no longer shows the time. In like manner, when a person chooses badly, he strays from his last end, abandons himself to disorderly affections, and renders his whole life a series of sins and misfortunes.

We must, therefore, carefully regulate this prime mover of life, whence all our actions proceed; otherwise, all our labors will be as hurtful as we believe them useful. A state of life that suits one person, may not suit another. A choice then, is a rule which serves us for measuring the lines of our actions, and for discovering whether they run directly to the end for which God created us, or diverge from it.

Listen to St. Gregory Nazianzen: *The choice*

3   25

of a state is the only foundation on which we can raise the edifice of a good or bad life. This is what faith taught St. Gregory. Seneca, guided by the light of reason alone, says: *Look to the whole tenor of your future life, for whatever you do must bear upon it: you will not manage well your particular affairs, unless you have in view your end.*

You see, that as soon as you choose your state, it serves to direct all your actions: they cannot be very prudent if they are not the offspring of the general choice which you may have made. "What think you," continues Seneca, " of a sailor, who puts to sea with sails unfurled, without having previously decided for what place he wishes to steer? You may say with reason, that he is foolish, and that probably his vessel will perish, since he does not even know which wind to desire, nor which is favorable, nor which opposed to reaching an end he knows not: indeed, since he knows not for what port to steer, no wind is favorable. But have you not just pronounced your own condemnation, if, without having made a good choice, you spread the sails of your hopes, permit every wind to drive, every current to hurry you away, without examining whether the course you pursue will lead you to bury your fortune in a gulf, or conduct you happily to a port?"

Let us add, that an error committed in the choice of a state is often without remedy, and it is therefore very important not to be deceived in it. A Spartan senator being asked, why he proceeded with so many precautions in capital sentences, replied: *Quia non est correctio errori."* "Because an error would be without remedy." When a very important affair cannot be recommenced, it should be attempted only after the greatest deliberation. The wise man says: *Adolescens juxta viam suam ambulans, etiam cùm senuerit non recedet ab ea:* "A young man according to his way, even when he is old, he will not depart from it." For instance, if a person undertakes commerce in his youth, he will continue it all his life, and will not even know how to leave it off. If he marries, death alone can break the bond; if to a bad woman, how much vexation will he not experience? A scanty fortune, and many children to provide for! What afflictions and troubles! If he embraces the ecclesiastical or religious state, once enlisted, he cannot recede; he must remain in it all his life. If it becomes displeasing, he may bewail his lot, but to change it is impossible. In fine, a man out of his state, is like a fish out of water, a bone out of joint; he lives in tribulation, in anguish, in continual solicitude; his labors, thoughts, and affections are filled with bitterness; and one bad action is the cause of another still worse.

SECTION 2. *A good choice gives a great hope of salvation.*

THE choice of a fit state not only influences the whole life, but also furnishes the chief means for obtaining eternal salvation.

St. Augustine and St. Thomas say, that the predestination of the elect is only the foreknowledge of God, and the disposal of the means by which He wishes to conduct the predestined to bliss. Now, the choice of a state is the chief means and the original source, whence are successively derived the other means for securing salvation. Divine wisdom having thus resolved from all eternity to give you existence and life, has at the same time decreed to plant in your heart from your earliest years that holy call. If it falls on a good soil, if you receive it with a ready will and correspond to it by choosing the state to which God calls you, you are happy, and your name is inscribed on the catalogue of the elect: you have found the first thread, and the first link in the chain of your predestination; the other means, like other links, will come in time, and join the first.

But if the heavenly seed does not find in you a good soil, if you are one of those who open the ear and not the heart to the voice of God, and who permit worldly ideas and sensual pleasures to stifle the thought of choosing the best, fear lest such conduct may cause your ruin, since you lose the chief and perhaps the only means of predestination. You derange the order of heavenly help and heavenly grace, which you need in order to save yourself; you run the risk of not reaching the true country, because you stray from the road. In running a swift race through the world, you make not a single step towards Heaven. St. Augustine will tell you, that, "you run well, but out of the way. He who does little, but in the state to which God calls him, does more than he who labors much, but in a state he has thoughtlessly chosen. A cripple limping in the right way, is better than a racer out of it."

Since the consequence of the choice will be either an eternal good or an eternal evil, is it prudent to delay repentance for having wandered, until repentance will be useless? The Holy Ghost warns us to do nothing without prudence: "*My son, do nothing unadvisedly.*" How much then of this prudence should we not use in the choice of a state of life, since this choice is the master-rule of all other actions! How deliberately ought we to proceed, that we may avoid an error without remedy, an evil in this life and in the

3 *

next. If there was ever an occasion on which might be said: "On one moment depends eternity," it is surely in choosing a state of life. If you are one of those who—like brutes—allow themselves to be carried away by passion, or—like slaves—are forced by the orders of a tyrant to embrace a state, apply to yourself the following advice: "*Audi, homo es, liber es, tuus es, de te agis. Elige ut homo, ut liber, ut tuus de te ipso benè age.* You are a man, free, and your own master. Show, by a wise choice, that you know well how to use the empire of reason and the dominion of liberty, in order to determine your life." The point is, to dispose of yourself wisely, in order to live happily, to die with confidence, and to save your soul; for such is the consequence of a good choice.

SECTION 3. *He who refuses to choose well exposes himself greatly to the danger of being damned.*

THE present subject is so important, that it must be presented in new and different lights. We read in Deuteronomy two remarkable promises: the one, in favor of those who obey God promptly: "*If you listen to the voice of your God, all blessings will come upon you.*" The other, against those who stubbornly refuse to receive heavenly inspirations: "*If you will not hear the voice of the Lord, all curses will come upon you; you will be cursed in the city, cursed in the country, &c."* You will also receive at the last judgment this terrible sentence: *" Depart, ye cursed, into everlasting fire."* What say you to this consequence? It is drawn from the threats of a God, infinitely true.

That you may understand how a bad choice produces a bad life, this life an unhappy death, and this death reprobation, I will clearly expose to you a theological truth. As divine Providence has given to men different characters and different qualities of mind and body, he has also established different states and different professions suited to these various dispositions. Moreover, He has from all eternity prepared graces suited to each state and to each man, in order to conduct him to salvation. So that all states are not adapted to every man, nor every state to all men: and God has not destined to all states the fulness of special and extraordinary graces, but reserves this for the state to which he calls a person.

If, therefore, you embrace a state of life, other than that to which God has inseparably attached these *particular* graces, you will receive only those which may, but which probably will not secure your salvation. In one moment you forfeit a most precious treasure of innumerable

graces, which would have made you victorious
in temptations. You lose, for the most part, the
three kinds of graces, which theologians call
protection, encouragement, and *direction,* of
which we have so great a need, that, were God
for one instant to turn away his eyes, and not
help us, we would be lost; like a little child that
walks because the nurse supports it, and would
fall, if for one moment left alone. By the first
of these graces, God defends us in our battles
against temptations, removes us from dangers,
and assists us after our falls. By the second, he
excites us to virtuous actions, pre-engages the
mind by his light, and moves the will by sweet
impulses. By the third, he directs us in the
midst of darkness and error, to the end that,
discerning good from evil, we may be able to flee
the one and practise the other. But he has been
pleased to attach to the state to which he calls
us, *the abundance of these three graces.* St.
Paul tells us, there are differences of graces, and
that God has destined to each man graces according to his vocation. " *Every one hath his proper
gift from God, one after this manner, and
another after that,*" (1 Cor. vii. 7;) and interpreters say, that this passage is applied to the
grace of vocation which a person has for one
state and not for another: for we cannot make
divine favors pass at our will from state to state.

"The virtue of the Holy Ghost, is given according to his order, not according to our will." (St. Cyprian.)

Behold how, in not embracing the state to which God calls you, you render yourself unworthy of the most precious blessings. Deprived of the particular protection of Heaven, your temptations will end in sins, your dangers in falls, and your falls in eternal ruin. Deprived of the lively impulse of exciting grace, you will not desire to embrace Christian virtues. Abandoned, and without the special direction of heaven, whither can you go in safety? How can you reach the haven of salvation? You will run the risk of yielding to your passions without remorse, of contracting bad habits without the hope of quitting them, of plunging into vice and continuing therein until death. God will abandon to you the reins, because you will not have obeyed his voice. *"But my people heard not my voice, and Israel hearkened not to me, so I let them go according to the desires of their heart. They shall walk in their own inventions."* (Ps. lxxx. 12.) Thus, man being rendered unworthy of divine favors, generally leads a life sullied with great and numerous sins, dies in horrible anguish of mind, and enters an unhappy eternity.

I will speak elsewhere of the punishment due

to those who resist God; and will only add here, that after the grace of baptism, which begins our life, and that of dying well, which ends it, the grace of choosing a state wisely is the most important and the most necessary of all graces; for it is the link or bridge which joins the grace of baptism to final grace, and over which we pass from a happy death to eternal life. It is like the keystone of an arch, because it sustains all the stones of the building, and the elect are *living stones built up into the temple of God.*

CHAPTER III.

SECTION 1. *He who has the greater talents has the greater obligation to choose well*

VERY man is obliged to make a good choice; but this obligation is the greater for him who has received from God greater gifts of nature and of grace. The greater the means which God grants to man, for obtaining his end, the greater the obligation to employ his efforts thereto. The servant who has received five talents, ought to gain far more than he to whom only one has been given; for the Evangelist says: *" To whom much is given, much shall be required of him."*

The more a land is favored by the sun, the more fruits and flowers it should bring forth. The shell that receives the more abundant dew, ought to afford the finer and more precious pearl. Thus, says St. Thomas, riches, nobility, and honors, are all motives exciting us to thankfulness; but a penetrating mind, a happy memory, eloquence, intelligence, and sound judgment are

85

so many spurs, urging us to gratitude to him from whom we have received them. But above all, we should correspond very faithfully to certain extraordinary favors of supernatural grace, when we are so fortunate as to receive them: for if we neglect to do this, we deserve, like the rebel angels, to be lost. Theologians think, that the chief reason which induced God to redeem fallen man, and not the fallen angels, was, that the angels, enriched by greater gifts of nature and of grace, all spiritual as they were, and living images of the Divinity, purposely wandered from their end, as if in contempt of the sovereign Benevolence.

Let us therefore bear in mind how great an evil it is, to employ in vain the talents God has so liberally bestowed upon us. He commits the most guilty theft, who takes what is most precious of the divine treasures, uses it for his pleasure, and pays no tribute from it to the Creator. St. Augustine says (Solil. 12): "He who seeks his own, not thy glory, O Lord, is a thief and a robber. He seeks to strip thee of thy glory, but deprives himself of an eternal reward." See then the great injury you offer God by abusing his favors, by misapplying the mind, which is a ray reflected from his divine countenance, and which ought to perform actions worthy of eternal glory! This is an affront that strikes his divine liberality to the heart; he resents it and complains sorrowfully of it by his holy Prophets: The children of Zion (Jer. Lam. iv.), enriched with gifts, adorned with the finest gold, with grace, destined to be vessels of honor, have become worldly vessels and vessels of shame. And elsewhere: "Children of men, how long will your hearts grow heavy? how long will you love vanity?" That is, how long shall I grieve to see those whom I have crowned with favors, abandon me to run after the false goods of the world? God condemns this ingratitude in a still more frightful manner (Ezek. xvi.): "*Thou tookest thy beautiful vessels of my gold and my silver, which I gave thee, and thou madest thee images of men.*" Thou hast usurped my gold, with which I adorned thee, and hast made of it idols to thy vanities. Thou hast profaned my gifts by sacrilegious abuses. Thou hast changed the treasures of my kindness into instruments which serve to insult me. Can you imagine a greater ingratitude?

The chastisements, with which God threatens the abuser of his gifts, are proportioned to his complaints. He even says, by his prophets, that there shall be a hell of special torments, which will correspond to the favors one may have despised. The greatest punishments are reserved for the ungrateful: the more favors a

4

person has received, the more guilty he is when he repays them with ingratitude?

Judge now, ye favored souls of heaven, if such a motive deserves to be seriously weighed in choosing a state. Hell is filled with brilliant minds, which, in this world, were instruments of vanity, and are now the prey of flames. God will demand of you a very strict account of his favors, of the talents, the learning, and the good dispositions with which he has adorned you in preference to others. He has given you an eagle-like greatness of soul, that you may soar towards heaven: then do not burrow in the earth like moles. God has impressed on your brow the luminous rays of his wisdom: do not trample them under foot, merely to raise yourself to vain honors. By perverting the use of so many good qualities, you derange the designs of divine Providence, and I leave you to conclude what your ingratitude will bring upon you, and what you must expect.

SECTION 2. *He who wishes to make the most of his talents, ought to make his choice well.*

Do not imagine, that in speaking of a choice, I wish to exact from you the highest degree of perfection. I will, however, show you that your temporal interests are also attached to a good choice; and that, without this choice, the greatest

gifts of nature and of grace can bring you no
great success even in the world. The mind is
undoubtedly of great value; but to misapply it,
is to bury in the dust a precious gem which was
designed to glitter in a royal crown. Wisdom
produces great advantages; but to obtain them
it must shine forth, and not be hidden under a
bushel. "To bury a talent under ground," says
St. Gregory, "is to employ in earthly concerns
the mind you received from God." (Hom. 9.)
How many youths, born for great undertakings,
lose their time in trifles, and give themselves up
to the torrent of vanity; whilst, if they labored
equally for things worthy of praise, they would
immortalize themselves, even in the estimation
of men!

Is this not doing much to little purpose? —
permitting the most precious talents to evapo-
rate in the smoke of ambition? Is it not imitating the folly of Nero, who tilled the earth
with a golden plough, and drove oxen with a
jewelled sceptre! A youth does far worse when
he employs a noble genius in vile pursuits. It
is heaping up riches for heirs, obtaining a title
— honorable but fruitless; growing lean over
books, to the neglect of more important affairs.
He may for a time abuse God's gifts, but will
soon be deprived of them.

God ordinarily takes his gifts from those who

abuse them.   Constantine passed this law : "If any one transfer his statues, columns, marble, &c., to the country, thus stripping the city of its ornaments, he shall be deprived of them." Ah ! your soul is that city, adorned with gifts so beautiful, enriched with jewels so precious ; and you have applied them to the convenience of your body.   Soon, however, you will forfeit them, for it is not my word but our Saviour's, *take the talent from him* which he has received from my liberality. For such abuses the fair daughter of Sion, that is, the soul beautified with graces, was deprived of her most admirable gifts ; and the Prophet Jeremiah weeps over her, saying : "All the beauty has departed from the daughter of Sion." (Lament. of Jer. i.)   But this is not all ; God often permits great talents to effect the ruin of those who abuse them.

Let us now consider those who have made a good use of their talents, and have gathered the fruit thereof.   Two brothers, born in poverty, had received from God very distinguished talents, and among other qualities, a soul-stirring eloquence : but there was a vast difference in the use they made of it.   One, having become a religious, preached in the most celebrated pulpits of Italy, spread the divine word, and was listened to with the greatest eagerness as a living oracle of the Holy Ghost.   The other, I know not by what whim, became a mountebank, and passed his life in acting comedies for a support. When he became incapable of this, he finished his unfortunate career in a hospital; representing really and in truth a most miserable tragedy. What a misfortune, to have employed so badly a gift which he might have used so well! "He was qualified by nature to do better things than he performed," as Quintilian said of Seneca. How did it happen that there was so great a difference between the twin brothers, who, in other respects, were so much alike? It was only the choice of a state, which conducted one to the temple of honor, and the other to an abode of misery.

St. Thomas of Villanova, of noble parentage, passed from the cloister to one of the chief Episcopal Sees of Spain; whilst his cousin remained in the world, at the plough, driving a yoke of oxen. Such was, for one and the other, the result of a choice.

Peter Faber, illustrious in the company of Jesus, was highly esteemed, not only by princes, cardinals and kings, who entrusted to him the cure of their souls, but by the greatest saints; such as St. Francis Xavier and St. Francis of Sales. Faber was born a poor countryman, in a hamlet of Savoy. He was the shepherd of a small flock, until the very moment he began his

4 *

studies. His talents were crowned with success. He repaired to the University of Paris, became a companion of St. Ignatius, chose wisely a life of perfection, and made such admirable progress in the road of wisdom and holiness, that the holy Bishop of Geneva, in his writings, honors him with the titles Blessed, great Director of Souls, and first Theologian of the Company of Jesus.

It is not only the wisdom of the saints which produces such wonderful effects; a single ray of judgment has directed a choice, and afterwards led to great virtues and great honors. Aulus Gellius relates of Protagoras, that in his youth he carried burdens to gain his living. One day, he returned from the woods with a burden which he could not have carried, had it not been so well arranged. The philosopher Democritus saw him, and considering the arrangement of the wood, and the ease with which he carried it, stopped him, and bade him undo the bundle, and make it over again in his presence. Protagoras obeyed. Democritus admired him, and concluded, that he had received from nature a mind capable of occupations very different from those of wood-carrier: consequently, he took him to his school, and made of him a celebrated philosopher. It is therefore true, that a good choice of a state has been of great assistance to many

men endowed with talents, who, coming from a
cabin, have been admired by the universe. It
has been with them as with vapors raised from
a marsh, and transformed into brilliant clouds.
This change is owing to the readiness with
which they permit themselves to be attracted by
the sun, which lifts them on high, even against
their nature. A bad choice, on the contrary,
causes many noble souls born for fortune to fall
into obscurity, like diamonds buried in the earth ;
which, if withdrawn from it, and polished, would
dazzle us with their admirable splendor.

Although the grace of God often works wonders by men of obscure birth, still, when it
endows certain noble souls, it seems to double
its strength — raising extraordinary minds for
extraordinary undertakings. Distinguished men
are generally more suited to great enterprises in
the service of God, provided they are docile and
have subdued their passions ; for then their heart
is a suitable temple for receiving the Holy Ghost.
Listen then to the words of the Prophet Eze-
kiel, addressed to those who have received from
God these precious qualities: "Every precious
stone was thy covering ; the sardius, the topaz,
and the jasper, the chrysolite, and the onyx, and
the beryl, the sapphire, and the carbuncle, and
the emerald ; gold the work of thy beauty,"

(xxviii. 13.)   God has been very liberal towards you, and requires in return a faithful correspondence on your part. Then make a choice worthy of your talents, which you are obliged to employ for the greater glory of him who has bestowed them upon you.

CHAPTER IV.

SECTION 1. *Extreme youth is not an obstacle to making a good choice.*

OME persons pretend, that the choice of a state is a step so important, that we ought to resolve upon it, only at an advanced age, when the judgment is perfectly ripe, and we have learned by experience all that takes place in the world. St. Thomas proves, however, that an affair so important ought surely to be decided before all others, and become the foundation-stone of all the projects you may form. If you have acquired the use of reason before the ordinary age, and are capable of discerning the end for which you are created, and the different roads that may conduct you to, or remove you from it, the holy Doctor advises you (op. 17, cii.) to anticipate the choice of your state. But as this case is rare, the holy church, enlightened by the Holy Ghost, has determined that at the age of fourteen a person is competent to judge for himself, and may embrace a state without awaiting the consent of his parents.

It is therefore very wrong, when any one, in contempt of Councils, (Trent Sess. 25,) blames a youth, (sixteen or eighteen years of age,) for having made his choice before his judgment was matured. Parents are guilty of injustice, when, by authority, cunning, threats, or flattery, they deprive children who have reached the prescribed age, of the liberty of choosing a state. Although they allege pretexts to justify their conduct, they are none the less guilty before God, of mortal sins, as the holy Doctors declare. St. Raymond experienced so great a remorse for having kept one of his relatives from entering religion, for having induced a soldier of the army of Jesus Christ to follow the standard of his enemy, that he did not believe himself able to atone for the injury done to God, except by entering the order himself, in the place of him whom he had kept away from it.

Youth is the most suitable age for making an excellent choice. It is the time most pleasing to God; and he promises particular graces to those who choose well in the opening of life. Read the eighth chapter of Wisdom — where God expressly says: "I, Wisdom, dwell in council, ... and they that watch for me early in the morning, shall find me." I am

Wisdom, I conduct those who walk with reflection. They who seek me in the morning of life, shall find me. God is not content with inviting, he orders: *My son, from thy youth up, receive instruction, and even to thy gray hairs thou shalt find wisdom.* (Eccl. vi. 18.) Then do not neglect it whilst heaven favors you with its light and blessings, for a little later this precious boon may elude your grasp. God also instructs youth by the example of a young man, who, because he took the road to perfection when very young, was so dearly beloved by our Saviour, as to cause the Apostles some jealousy. If the flower of age is not sullied by worldly pleasures, it is an object of special blessing and delight to God. A pure young heart, free from the roots of evil, offers the celestial Gardener a soil ready for receiving the dews of good thoughts which produce great actions. A mind, not darkened by the clouds of passion, is best prepared for receiving the rays of the divine Sun, which enable it to distinguish what is truly good from what is so in appearance only.

This light and truth have caused the most celebrated men to choose their states in tender youth; and they did it with more than the maturity of age. St. Thomas Aquinas, St. Aloysius, St. Bennet, and St. Anthony, (names ever glorious,) resolved before the age of fifteen to abandon the world, and enlist under the standard of Jesus. Other heroes of the Church, St. Charles Borromeo, St. Philip Neri, and St. Francis of Sales, from their earliest youth, despised the great hopes the world offered, and consecrated the flower of life to God in the ecclesiastical state. But one of the most remarkable was St. Antoninus, bishop of Florence, who, hardly thirteen years of age, resolved to give himself to God in the order of St. Dominic.

God showed by a prodigy how pleasing this youthful offering was to him. Antoninus, on the one side, was impatient to assume the religious habit; and the Prior, on the other, fearing too much precipitation, deferred his admission, and asked what he was studying. "The canon law," replied Antoninus. "Well," said the Prior, "when you know all the Canons and Decrees by heart, return, and I will receive you." He felt sure that several years would roll by before Antoninus could succeed. The high-minded youth joyfully accepted the condition, and at the end of the first year called on the Prior for the fulfilment of his promise. He answered a very severe examination so well as to astonish all the assistants, and was received into the order as a treasure sent from heaven.

SECTION 2. *Abundant fruits destined for those
who choose in time.*

*To the ingenuous youth Fulco; Brother Ber-
nard, greeting: That only will cheer him in youth,
which he will not repent of in old age.* Such
was the address of a letter from St. Bernard, to
a youth who inquired how he should employ his
early years. Spend your youth in such a manner, that when you become an old man, you will
not regret the use you may have made of it. It
would be an irreparable loss, if you should await
the experience of many years before making a
choice. You would be foolishly losing the precious time given you to begin what you must
follow during your whole life. Does a laborer
spend half the day in examining whether he
shall work in the fields or in the vineyard?
Does a banker keep his treasures locked up for
years, reflecting how he shall use them to advantage? Ought we, therefore, delay putting
to a good use the talents which the divine bounty
has bestowed upon us? We would only deserve
the sentence pronounced against the slothful
servant who hid the money his master gave him
to use: "Take the talent from him, and cast this
useless servant into outer darkness." He who
opens not his eyes to the light of the Holy
Spirit, deserves to be deprived of it, and to be

5

cast into darkness, never again to receive that light so necessary for finding the true road to salvation.

Jesus wept over Jerusalem, because this unfortunate city did not know the time of its visitation; as if not to profit in time of divine favors, and to plunge into utter ruin, were one and the same thing: The day will come when thou shalt be desolate, *and they shall not leave in thee a stone upon a stone.* (St. Luke xix. 44.) The Wise man tells us, that as flowers and fruits appear in the season assigned to them, so every enterprise should be carried out in its suitable time. St. Augustine, St. Jerome, and St. Thomas, all say, that the proper time for choosing a state is the earliest youth.

Listen to a philosopher blaming those who waste the morning of life, and reserve manhood as the best time for making a choice. " Can one imagine," says Seneca, " in the self-same being, a lavishness and an avarice more out of place and more hurtful, than when a person spends his youth in wickedness, and reserves the worst years for a better life? It is the most precious and the strongest liquor, that comes first from a vessel, whilst the dregs remain at the bottom: thus it is with the life of man; the first years are years of more sprightliness and ardor; and shall we spend them without any profit, and give to perfection the miserable dregs of old age? This would be imitating the cunning actor, who, in his youth, when he could please spectators, declaimed in public, but in his old age, when he could not please them, withdrew to the capitol, and acted his comedies before the gods, saying: "Now all shall be done for the gods, and nothing for men." Then, weigh well in your mind this sentence: *Optima quæque dies miseris mortalibus ævi prima fugit.* Why is youth the best time? Because it is then easier to form a docile and tractable mind to virtue and perfection. Happy he, who in his tender years, has learned to bear the yoke of virtue. He walks better in his path, when early accustomed to it. Grace seems changed into nature, and nature into grace. St. Thomas says, that in tender years, one is more flexible, more capable of receiving the impressions of the Holy Spirit; and having received them, is more capable of always preserving them. Aristotle says: "It is very important that one habit or another be taken in early years; all the rest depends on this. It is with men, as with plants: when young, they easily take any direction, but when they grow hard, they cannot be straightened."

SECTION 3. *The great dangers of those who delay their choice.*

WHEN a person defers his choice until an advanced age, if unfortunately a vice takes root in his tender heart, how difficult to destroy it! A young man too easily forms a bad habit: the weakness of his age, the scandals he sees, the example of his young companions, the ardor of his blood, all give grounds for fear; and God only knows when he will correct himself. It is still more frightful, if he is exposed to sensual pleasure, which, once tasted, gives so terrible a craving for it, that, like poison drunk in milk, it quickly spreads through all the veins, and causes evils often incurable. This is the sin into which young persons so easily fall, and of which they can rid themselves, in after-life, only by great struggles. The mind becomes blind when seeking remedies, the will feeble in adopting them: they learn, but too late, that this vice is a narrow well, into which they easily fall, but from which they escape only with struggles and great help.

We cannot conquer this sin, without extraordinary favors from heaven. The Apostles received power over all those possessed by devils, except such as were possessed from their infancy, to let us know that particular grace is necessary to uproot a vice contracted in youth. St. Augustine says, that paths of vice are inclined and covered with ice. It is easy for children to start along them, but having once started, it is no longer in their power to stop or return. " *Their way becomes dark and slippery.*" (Ps. xxxiv. 6.) A bad habit causes a sort of necessity, and when it is requisite to get clear of it, there is a lack of will very like a want of strength. By the first faults, a youth willingly sells himself as a slave to sensuality ; little by little he becomes ensnared, and finds himself forever bound by heavy chains, a galley-slave to vice.

But even if by a singular privilege you shall be preserved from iniquity, as you advance in years you will find yourselves burdened with a thousand affairs, with the care of a family, with the administration of wealth, perhaps with civil affairs, and will no longer even think of choosing a state. Imagine yourself standing before a vast labyrinth, with thousands of winding pathways, and before entering, reflect and choose: *Hic stans delibera.*

5*

CHAPTER V.

SECTION 1. *What are the good and the bad dispositions for making a choice?*

NE of the most necessary dispositions for choosing well, is, without doubt, a perfect indifference. He who begs of God to know his will regarding any thing, ought beforehand to break his attachments and strip himself of all inclinations to this side or that; afterwards generously to place himself in the hands of his Divine Majesty, and be ready to do whatever may please Him. Many persons have not this indifference, because they do not understand what God would do with him who should place himself entirely in his hands, and be ready to go whithersoever his grace might call him. A shapeless mass of marble would never believe itself capable of becoming a wonder of sculpture; and if it could, it would never give itself up to the workman's chisel. And so it is with those who wish to impede the hand of God; they permit him to dispose of them up to a certain point, but not

entirely ; and sometimes they are already decided not to embrace this or that state They
would wish to lay down laws to the Holy Ghost,
as if a pilot should command the wind to blow
always aft, and refuse to receive it from any
other quarter. Others, still more senseless, undertake their choice, but are already inclined to
embrace some particular state ; like a seaman
who would spread his sails to the wind, having
previously cast anchor to fix his vessel. Such
persons have double work to do ; first, to put
out of their mind what has been planted in it by
caprice, and afterwards to introduce what is conformable to reason.

It is therefore necessary before making a
choice, to acquire this indifference, which, says
St. Thomas, consists in having the affections
well balanced, so that you may have neither dis-
like nor inclination to any particular state of
life, and may await the slightest touch from the
finger of God, to start you in your proper path.
It would be still better to present your mind to
God, as a sheet of white paper, upon which he
may write whatever is his pleasure. That is,
you should have in your mind, neither whim nor
determination. Prejudices have great inconveniences ; for they ingraft themselves on the
affections and resolutions of the will. Therefore, make your mind and heart perfectly calm,

and say: "my heart is ready, Lord, to execute thy adorable will." But say it with all sincerity, and do not be like the young man who asked Jesus: "Master, what shall I do to be saved?" What indifference! What readiness! The Lord kindly replied to him: "If you wish to enter into life, keep the commandments." But the young man added: "I have always kept them; what still remains?" The Saviour replied: "If you will be perfect, sell your goods, give the price thereof to the poor, come and follow me." These words were like a thunderbolt to him, and he retired full of sadness. Where now is his indifference! He was wedded to his riches; said one thing, and thought another. How many young persons pretend to seek the will of God, and are already determined to follow their own fancy! How many say, "Lord! what shall I do?" and wish Christ to reply: "What do you wish I should tell you to do? to what state of life do you wish that I should call you?" This is not the way to serve God on earth, and obtain a great reward in Heaven.

SECTION 2. *Inconstancy is a great obstacle to making a good choice.*

IT is a great obstacle, in choosing a state, to be inconstant. An inconstant soul turns to every breeze, is incapable of great undertakings, wishes all things, but embraces nothing. To acquire great virtue, it is necessary to aim continually at a single object. An inconstant soul is not capable of this; he thinks about every thing, and decides upon nothing: " They wander without any purpose, seeking for business, and they do not what they have purposed." Important affairs demand reflection and constancy. A student, who flutters over all sciences, learns none. An oft removed tree produces few flowers and but little fruit. The Wise man says to us: *Winnow not with every wind, and go not into every way ;* but abhor fickleness, and be constant in all your actions, so that you may say: *Pes meus stetit in directo.*

Inconstancy in the young, is a fever, peculiar to their age; passions continually agitate them, and their mind is always turned topsy-turvy by new desires and consequent restlessness: they wish to rest whilst at work, and work when at rest. Like quicksilver, they are continually moving. If engaged with the choice of a state, they glance at all states and stop at none. If we wish to settle them, that they may receive the rays of heavenly light, they are seen to change like the plumage of a dove in the sunbeams, whose color we cannot tell because it shows all colors. They consider all states and

embrace none. Speak to them of the study of
law, they are all readiness; but, the next minute,
they will think of the religious or ecclesiastical
state, and will have a great desire to embrace it,
which will vanish as soon as they think of another state. They resemble the chameleon's
skin, which takes the color of all surrounding
objects. The Wise man says of inconstancy:
"The heart of a fool is as the wheel of a cart,
and his thoughts are like a rolling axle-tree."
(Ecc. xxxiii. 5.) How is it possible to make a
wise choice with such a disposition?

St. Ambrose, exhorting young persons to
constancy, says: "Accustom yourselves to be
always the same, that your conduct may seem
like a painting, which presents always the same
appearance." Seneca had before said, that, uni-
formity of conduct is a great virtue; it can only
be found in a wise man: he who has it not,
often changes, and it is this that hinders him
from doing anything truly great.

You will say that I know your disease very
well, and will ask me the cure for this giddiness.
I give you that which naturalists prescribe for
stopping quicksilver, which is always in motion
until it meets gold, with which it unites, and
from which it receives solidity. I will tell you
to fix your heart on God, because St. Augustine
says: "He who fixes his heart on an immovable

object becomes immovable." But how will you succeed in this! The following practices will contribute to it.

1. Enter seriously into yourself, seek the source whence this uneasiness proceeds, and remove the cause to hinder the effect.

2. Select some acts of virtue to. practice, and let them be always the same; for by choosing sometimes one and sometimes another, you do not cure, but aggravate inconstancy. It weakens a sick person to be continually changing the remedy

3. Choose a prudent confessor who knows your infirmity, and follow his treatment. The woman of the Gospel, who was ailing for many years had had many physicians and different remedies, yet she went from bad to worse.

4. Arrange with your confessor the order of all the actions of the day, and make a good resolution of observing it as exactly as possible.

5. If, after your resolutions, you still commit faults, do not be impatient; do not think you will never obtain constancy because you do not succeed at first, but correct your faults manfully, put the present in order, and provide for the future.

CHAPTER VI.

SECTION 1. *He deceives himself who believes, that, to make his choice, and to leave the world, are one and the same thing.*

AS soon as you perceive the end you ought to have in view in making your choice, you are seized with a frightful panic, like a child at the sight of a ghost. If I ought, say you, to choose a state only with the light of eternal truths and the maxims of the Gospel, farewell my home, farewell my parents; riches, places, all farewell! I must, whether I will or not, turn my back upon the world, and hasten into a cloister. I am not ready for it; my mind directed by prudence will lead me towards employments suitable to my birth: after all, my family is not so perverse that I cannot find God in remaining with it. Honors are not so dangerous that they necessarily tend to my ruin. Therefore, why should I crack my skull in thinking of a choice? I would draw from it no other fruit, than to raise in my mind a tempest of scruples and uneasiness! Moreover, I might conclude that I ought to be a religious, and perhaps I would not have the resolution to become one; I have too great a repugnance to it; I cannot even think of it without becoming sad. Moths, in fluttering around the light, are sure to singe their wings. I prefer then to remain in my simplicity: for when one wishes to know too much, it sometimes happens that he learns what he would wish never to have known.

Have you nothing more to say? Have at least the patience to listen to my reply. In the first place, I would say, that you resemble Marcian, who refused to read the Holy Scriptures, for fear of finding a refutation of his errors. Now, I will reply with St. Bernard: all that hinders you from seeking the will of God is, that you imagine you will find nothing but rigor there, where all is love. Know then, that if your desire is upright and favorable to your salvation, God is so good that he will conform himself to what will please you. This is why the prophet calls divine grace a voluntary rain, that is, according to the interpreters, a rain that accommodates itself to the will. St. Cyril remarks on this subject, that grace acts on our wills like a gentle rain on gardens; it conforms to the good dispositions of the ground, whitens

6

on the lily and reddens on the rose. In the
same manner, the grace of God bends itself to
the good inclinations of men, and seconds their
good wishes. But if your desire is hurtful to
you, why cling to what may cause your perdition? God does not invite you to any state
for the good he may receive from it, but only
with a view to your own interest. If you do
not listen to him, it is to yourself you do the
injury. Moreover, you deceive yourself, when
you think, that making a good choice is the
same thing as quitting the world. God has expressly ordained that some should remain there
for his glory. He has from all eternity decreed,
that his Church should be composed of all kinds
of saints, like a garden which becomes more
agreeable by the variety of the flowers it contains. Providence establishes various states,
and conducts different men to the same end by
different roads.

If you read the Holy Court of Father Caus-
sin, you will see that the Holy Ghost has been
pleased that some should enter armies to defend
the interests of their country, that others should
apply themselves to the study of law to keep the
balance of justice aright, that all should present
great models of virtue, whether in the army or
at the bar.

I will cite you one example out of a thousand.

Count Elzear having been brought up in the peaceful retreat of a monastery, experienced a lively grief when he was afterwards exposed to the turmoils of a court; and he was afflicted the more, because, in an ecstasy, he had clearly seen the excellence of eternal goods, and the baseness of temporal things. Once, prostrate at the foot of his crucifix, he poured forth this touching lament: "My God, I have received great favors from thy infinite goodness: I acknowledge that it is to this I owe the happiness of having preserved my chastity. But these treasures of grace are exposed to great dangers, for I carry them in a vessel of clay amid the tumults of the world. At the court I must continually live in battles, where struggles are common and victories rare; where vice finds a welcome home, and virtue is found only by miracle. I care little for having lost my repose, but am pained for always placing thy honor in danger; grant me, Lord, the light and strength I need, to withdraw myself to a hermitage, where I will be removed from the world and the danger of offending thee: there, I would serve thee with all my heart, I would enjoy thy graces, I would thank thee for thy gifts." Thus he prayed, when God clearly replied to him: "I do not wish you to abandon the court: I am pleased that you should dwell there: I have never wished you to re-

nounce your riches, but to make a good use of
them at your pleasure." The Count, astonished
at this reply, added with renewed ardor: "My
God, I see so many precipices before me that I
dare not make a single step. How can I always
preserve myself amid them? Thou knowest
how very weak I am." God replied to him,
that by His powerful grace, He would supply
the deficiency of his strength, and thus enable
him to preserve the treasure of chastity. After
this heavenly vision, as if his soul had been
created anew, he began to live in the world, as
though he were not of the world; and all that
did not lead towards God, was as nothing to
him.

He passed all his life, so occupied with his
own and the public good, that he was at once a
Count and a Religious. God does not therefore
call all men to the cloister: there are some whom
he calls to the world; and to these he grants
powerful helps to conduct themselves well therein.

SECTION 2. *We always follow the invitation of
God with pleasure, and never refuse without
committing a fault.*

I WILL suppose for a moment, that God calls
upon you to leave the world. You fear that
thereby he opposes your inclinations, and only
grieves you. "Do not deceive yourself," says

St. Augustine; "do not believe that God will draw you against your will; the heart is drawn by love. God will enlighten your mind and touch your heart with sweetness, in such a manner that you will be led, not only willingly, but also with pleasure: "Pleasure leads every one," says the Lord. You will hasten to God willingly and with joy. As a lamb follows you, when you show it a green branch, so, when God gives you sufficient light, your heart will experience more contentment in flying from the world, than it now finds in indulging the hope of honors and riches. It will be with you as with the three Wise Kings, who followed with great joy the star that guided them to Jesus. "In fact," says St. Thomas, "when God enlightens the mind of man, and makes him know the good an object contains, he at the same time sweetly inclines the will to love it, and to seek it with hope, or at least with desire. From the time you are willing to know and think of it, you find your delight in loving it; for God, in the operations of his grace, always mingles sweetness with strength. By his gifts, he raises nature to esteem even difficult things; but he never does violence, to make you practise by force, what you regard as hateful.

If God dispels the darkness and permits you to see the beauty of virtue, if he changes the

6*

longing of your heart so that you will have more relish for a great good than for a small one, will you not cherish the greater? If what you seek after as gold, were proved not to be genuine, would you not renounce it to acquire the true virgin gold? If you would not, you resemble a leper who refused to be cured because it was agreeable to him to be able to beg by the aid of his disease, which excited compassion. You are one of those foolish persons who prefer darkness to light. I say more: if you refuse the light necessary to a wise choice, your ignorance is very culpable: you say to God, nearly in the words of the impious man cited in Job, "*Remove from us your rays, O Father of light, we are resolved to shut our eyes to the light which shows us the good way.*" Expect then the chastisements which these impious men received; calamities of every kind in this life as a prelude to the eternal misery of the next. "It can never go well with a man who, having left God's guidance, prefers listening to his own counsels." Your ignorance is gross—as theologians call it. — It springs not from a natural defect, but from voluntary negligence, which makes your errors wilful, and proves your loss to be your own work. You are obliged to seek the will of God, for a servant is bound to inform himself of his master's will, as well as to execute it when known. If you fail to do this you are guilty, and it must be said of you as of the impious Belthazzar : " He would not understand that he might do well."

This ignorance is not only gross but pretended, and expressly affected. You are always on your guard lest a good thought may enter your mind ; you act the sentinel to keep the will of God from the door of your heart. If a spark of truth unexpectedly appears, you divert yourself with amusements. You would wish to steal away from the penetrating eye of God and boldly reply to him in the day of judgment : " *I have not known thy ways.*" " What ! did you not know my ways," God will reply ; and why have you not sought them ? Why have you shut your eyes that you might not see ? I know you not : depart into the darkness you have so eagerly sought.

CHAPTER VII.

SECTION 1. *When is a person to follow his inclination, and when not?*

HY, you will ask, employ so much care in the choice of a state, if each one should yield to the sweet violence of his inclinations? Every man is born with a natural propensity which urges his will to one state or to another. Whoever does not follow his inclination, acts by constraint, and can never succeed. No one is suited to a state opposed to his natural liking; this liking therefore is the only rule we ought to follow.

I admit that a person ought to follow his inclination, but would you not wish at least to look thoroughly into yourself, and learn for what state your dispositions best suit you? The Wise man counsels this. (Eccl. xxxvii.) When you make a choice, examine — with care — for what you are best suited, and to what inclined; for all states do not suit every man. The Athe-

nians, when the time came for teaching an art
to young men, made them examine the instruments used in the different professions, explained
to them their advantages and difficulties, and
believed those youths best suited to that profession or trade whose tools they handled with the
greatest pleasure and skill.   Do the same with
your thoughts, in order to ascertain for what
state you are best adapted; and afterwards, with
the help of God, embrace the state in which you
hope to succeed best.   But, beforehand, listen to
two important counsels which St. Gregory the
Great gives you:

First; you ought not to follow your inclination, when it leads you to certain states that are
dangerous, and much exposed to vice.

These professions are sufficiently numerous —
*sunt pleraque negotia, quæ sine peccatis exhiberi,
aut vix aut nullatenus possunt.*   I will not name
them, continues the saint, but will only say in
general, that there are states, in which ambition
leads to flattery, falsehood, envy, and under-
valuing your rivals; in which avarice excites to
perjury, violence, and robbery; in which you
may have to sustain a false point of honor by
crimes, or continually attend feasts and plays;
professions, which you know perhaps better
than I.   When you feel drawn to such states,
you ought not to follow your inclination, but

should replace it by a wise choice; otherwise you evidently risk your salvation. It is better to move with oars, and reach a place of safety, than with all sails set, to be carried to shipwreck.

Secondly; when your inclination leads you to a state morally honest, it is not enough to consider that willing delight, and sweet bent of nature towards it; it is still necessary to examine seriously what accompanies this state, to compare the good with the evil you may expect to find, the safeguards or dangers it offers to salvation, the hardships and pleasures, the successes and reverses, generally met with therein. Your desires will sometimes lead you, with natural impetuosity, to a state somewhat dangerous; and again, with less force, but by more reasonable motives, to another state less perilous. Then, concludes the Saint, embrace that state in which there is less risk. Be persuaded that in this state, your inclination will help you the more, as plants removed to a more favorable soil, produce more fruit. It is certainly necessary to seek good trees, but it is still more essential to place them in good soil, where those that are common will become excellent. "It is the soil, not the vine, that tempers the grape;— for the same vine brings forth different grapes in a different ground." It is certain, that the kind of life does a great deal towards turning natural dispositions to good or to evil.

St. Gregory, the theologian, in his admirable epistle to Eudoxius, the rhetorician, shows that the manner of choosing a state amongst Pagans, is very different from that amongst Christians. The Pagans embraced at will the state they believed most suitable to their talents and birth; but we cannot content ourselves with so little, because, enlightened by faith, we know better what are the virtues to be practised in this life, in order to be eternally happy in the next. We must follow our inclination, so long as it leads towards heaven, but when it does not, we must oppose it: for " *The kingdom of heaven suffereth violence, and the violent bear it away.*" (Matt. xi. 12.) The Saints purchased heaven by their toil and their blood; shall we hope to obtain it without any suffering, and by doing only what pleases us? Besides, we ought to rely, not only upon the helps of nature, but also upon those that are supernatural, which often give us grace so efficacious, that we succeed in things for which we thought ourselves unfit; for Divine Providence sometimes performs wonderful actions by means of men without talent.

But since it is useful to know and follow this genuine natural inclination, let us preserve it as far as possible; changing, however, its matter,

or at least its intention. I will explain myself.
St. Ignatius had inclinations wholly warlike; he
made use of his generous dispositions to estab-
lish a new company of soldiers, and to compose
that famous meditation of the "Two Standards;"
the one raised by Jesus Christ, the other by
Lucifer. He therefore preserved his inclination,
but applied it to another warfare. Alexander of
Ales was naturally fond of study, but he employed his talent in the continual study of the
Holy Scriptures and mystic theology : he preserved the inclination, but changed its matter.
St. Chrysostom abandoned the eloquence of the
bar, to embrace that of the pulpit. St. Romuald
was given to the chase. In his very hunting-
grounds he led a hermit's life, and "there did
he seek his God." You will find many examples
of it in all states. Then carefully consider by
what means you can follow your inclination,
and, at the same time, embrace an honest state,
which will lead you to virtue.

SECTION 2. *A bad inclination can be rectified
and reformed by virtue.*

WE see men by nature so perverse, and so far
removed from good, that they seem unfit for any
state in which the least virtue is required. Must
we abandon them, and give them no remedy?
One would sometimes be tempted to do this, for

it is very difficult to conquer a harsh nature.
Often, however, it is easier to cure than is generally believed, provided, we undertake it with
courage, and are confident of success. St. Bernard, the great physician of souls, assures us,
that he has seen persons who were obstinate and
reckless, become, with the help of reason and
religion, truly obedient and mild. Demosthenes,
born a stammerer, and awkward in whatever he
did, seemed more suited, like his father, to the
trade of a blacksmith than to the exercises of
the forum. However, he took so much care in
correcting his extraordinary natural defect, that
we see in him quite another man. He became
the first of orators ; so that Valerius Maximus
wittily observes: "The mother brought forth
one Demosthenes, and industry another."

But since natural diligence is so powerful,
what will it not be when aided by supernatural
grace ? St. Ignatius was naturally passionate
and impetuous; the physicians believed he was
of a cold and melancholy disposition, because
they attributed the deadness of his passions to a
natural coldness, which was only the effect of a
continued effort to subdue the fire of his anger.
It is for this he warns us, that he who is naturally reckless and can endure no restraint, ought
not to lose hope, nor believe himself unfit for
any virtuous state, but should correct himself

7

with energy. If he succeeds in conquering his evil dispositions, he will be very suitable for great undertakings in the service of God. His ambition, directed towards spiritual things, will not be content with ordinary labors, but will be like a tamed lion, which preserves its courage, after having lost its ferocity. Vice more easily abides in a soul that seems dead and immovable.

Aristotle says, that the passions ought not to be absolutely destroyed, but only disarmed and corrected; because, when reduced to obedience, they admirably assist us in the practice of the most heroic virtues. He proves that passions assist us in undertaking great things, and therefore does not wish them to be exterminated, but to be treated as a wild horse, that is, to be tamed and broken to the bit. These passions, once subjected to reason, will be very useful to him who knows well how to command them. Let us imitate the gardener, who takes a wild and thorny shrub, joins to it a small graft, and thus makes it bear delicious fruit. The root does not change its nature, but the fruits of the tree are improved, because it makes a better use of the sap: *Miraturque novas frondes, et non sua poma.* It will be the same with a perverse nature, whose productions are vicious; if you cultivate it with care, and ingraft virtues on it, you will see good and virtuous actions spring into life. St. Paul expresses the same under this allegory: Cut out of the wild olive tree, and, contrary to nature, grafted into the good olive tree. (Rom. xi. 24.) St. Augustine compares the nature of men to that of plants, and concludes, that, by means of a graft, we can produce delicious fruit from a bad root. To him, whose inclinations are directly opposed to virtue, I do not say: "Embrace at once a state which exacts tranquillity and obedience," with a hope that he will soon correct himself. For example, I do not advise a man of a violent temper: "To clothe himself with an ecclesiastical habit without delay;" supposing him from that time to approach the altar, and there offer a holocaust of all his disordered passions. No; I wish only to warn you, that, if you aspire to a good choice, you must, beforehand, and without awaiting an advanced age, correct your bad inclinations, and reduce to the empire of reason whatever rebels against it. I only encourage you to seize the remedy, and use it with patience, so that, little by little, it may cure you. You will doubtless wish and hope for success, if you consider the happiness of a heart that is obedient to reason, free from the agitation of passion, and always enjoying a perfect calm. How pleasing is that heavenly peace of mind, which is never disturbed by harrowing thoughts, that gentleness of manners which conciliates love, that perfect harmony which produces serene joys! These will be the fruits of the victory you will have won over yourself; for, to conquer corrupt nature is to uproot disordered passions, which are ever the parent of sadness, and to replace them by virtuous habits, the only sources of the spiritual delights which God bestows on those who fight the good fight: "To him that overcometh, I will give the hidden manna." (Apoc. ii. 17.) If you are pleased with this result, take yourself in hand, and boldly enter upon the reform of whatever one your nature contains.

CHAPTER VIII.

SECTION 1. *Of a bad choice founded on human motives.*

NE of the greatest mistakes a youth can make is to embrace a state without making a prudent choice; that is, to be guided by natural impulse, by the desire of riches, or by the force of passion. In the first place, St. Ambrose observes, that many young persons adopt a state, only because it is that of their father, of which we see frequent examples in all conditions of life. And relatives often go so far as to persuade, and even force, children to do this. When one is an only son, the sentence is passed; he must marry, in order to keep up the family. If God calls elsewhere, heavenly laws must yield to worldly interests. If there are several children, they are irrevocably divided between God and the world, but, of course, the world has the preference. The eldest must marry a rich wife; another study law; another devote himself to medicine. Finally, another must try his fortune

in war, and he may escape its perils as best he can. The daughters are disposed of in the same manner. Behold the plans of a wise father of a family, or, rather, of a perfidious murderer of his offspring; not of their bodies, but, what is worse, of their souls!

But young persons, who have a little good sense and nobleness of heart, ought not to permit their parents to exercise such a despotism over their choice of a state, as if they were the sovereign judges of vocations, and the oracles of the Holy Spirit. There are often considerable differences between the natural dispositions of the father, and those of his children: why, then, ought they to have the same state? When the son falls sick, why do they call a physician who examines his case? Would it not be better to give him simply the remedies which once entirely cured the father? You will say that this would be a folly, because their constitutions are different. But is it not the greatest of follies, to wish to lead to eternal salvation, by the same road, both father and son, whose natural dispositions are more opposed than fire and water? The father of St. Francis was a wealthy merchant; the son was, however, chosen by God to give the world an example of the greatest poverty. Gonzaga was a courtier, but Aloysius, his eldest son, was called by heaven to the

humility of a religious order. Charles II.—
king of Naples—was a warlike prince; but God
inspired St. Louis, his son, the heir of three
crowns, to refuse the sceptre, and enlist under
the standard of the cross. The father of St.
Francis of Sales was a soldier, but the son was
chosen by the Holy Ghost to wear the mitre,
and be an example to all ecclesiastics. If these
heroes in sanctity had followed in the footsteps
of their fathers, perhaps they would not now be
in heaven, and their names would not have
acquired that celebrity on earth which they
now enjoy. God, wishing to make a great hero
of Abraham, said to him: *Go forth out of thy
country and from thy kindred, and out of thy
father's house, and I will bless thee, and I will
magnify thy name.*

SECTION 2. *Family interest ought not to influence
us in choosing.*

WORLDLY wisdom employs still another argument, more reasonable in appearance, but equally
false. An only son ought to be the prop of his
family. A poor argument this! A young Nea-
politan, an only son, had resolved to leave the
world; his father, by a cruel tenderness, left no
means untried to change his mind, and offered
him the most advantageous alliance, in order
thereby to prevent the extinction of his family.

The poor young man yielded, but, after a month's marriage, an illness of several days carried him off without his leaving any successor to his name. See what results from embracing a state against the will of God. "There is no wisdom, there is no prudence, there is no counsel, against the Lord." (Prov. xxi. 30.) When God calls, all other considerations must be set aside; and, if a person wishes to reason, he should say: "This is an only son, but, since he cannot be divided between God and the world, it is but just that he should be entirely God's." This is an only son: it is then to be feared, that, seeing himself an heir to a considerable fortune, he may employ it in offending God, and thereby lose an eternal inheritance.

St. John the Baptist, of the princely house of Zachary, wished, from his infancy, to flee into the desert, in order to preserve in its purity the lily of his virginity, and was not deterred by the thought that this step terminated a family of the chosen people of God, as ancient as illustrious. St. Alexis, the only son of a Roman prince, crowned with honors and riches, left all, the very night of his wedding, without allowing the displeasure of his parents, or the extinction of his family, to hold him back. Fabius, a Roman knight, the last descendant of the renowned Fabii of ancient Rome, buried their glory in a religious life. To those who proposed to obtain for him a dispensation from his vows that he might continue a family so glorious to Rome for more than two thousand years, he replied, that he thought nothing more honorable to his family than to end in a man entirely consecrated to the glory of God.

Your family is, perhaps, not more distinguished than those just named : why fear so much to give so honorable an end to your ancestral line, which will perpetuate their glory in a happy eternity? A youth, the only son of parents far advanced in years, ardently desired to embrace a religious life, but his parents wished absolutely that he should keep up their name. To obtain his liberty, he addressed the Queen of Angels with so many and such fervent prayers, that his parents were blessed with a second son. He then renewed his entreaties, which were crowned with success, and became a most distinguished religious. An only child receives from God signal favors when he forms noble resolutions and despises worldly hopes. The Holy Scriptures teach us that God · showered abundant blessings on Abraham's family, because this Patriarch consented to sacrifice his only son: *" Because thou hast not spared thy only-begotten son for my sake, I will bless thee, and I will multiply thy seed as the stars of heaven; and in thy seed shall all the nations of the earth be blessed, because thou hast obeyed my voice.*" (Gen. xxii.)

Even when a father has more children than St. Leopold, who was blessed with eighteen, he has not on that account the right to bargain with God, and distribute them in such a manner that one shall sustain the family, others become soldiers, ecclesiastics, religious, etc.; but he should say to them with that wise Prince, "Choose what you please; see whom you ought to serve, in order to save your souls." The Machabees were seven brothers, and they were all called to the army. In the house of St. Basil there were four brothers; all became religious, very celebrated Bishops, and, what is more, great Saints. St. Bernard, the scion of a most distinguished family, had six brothers; all of them left the world, to enter a monastery. When several of them were on their way, they met their youngest brother — Nivardo — who was playing in the street with his school-fellows. "Brother," said Guido, the eldest, "good-bye; we are going to the monastery; we have left you all our property." At these words the child cried out, "What! you take heaven for yourselves, and leave me the earth! No; that is not fair. I, too, have sufficient courage to despise so worthless an inheritance."

He immediately followed his brothers, and all had the happiness of forming a new brotherhood in the same monastery. Therefore, when heaven gives a father several children, he ought not to dispose of them in different states, merely according to his interest or his caprice. This depriving others of their liberty is an act of deliberate injustice. Men ought not to make such bargains with God, but each one should say— "My lot is in thy hands."

SECTION 3. *Worldly hopes ought not to direct a choice.*

ANOTHER error, no less dangerous, is to choose a state with a view to self-interest only. This is the sole object of those who are called "promising youths," who build castles in the air, and imagine that they will soon possess a fortune and preferments, which they will never obtain. "Credulous youth," says Louis the Just, "imagines itself in the centre of the city—when it can barely hear its distant bells." How deceitful are your hopes! You imitate Æsop's dog, which, in endeavoring to seize the shadow of the meat in the water, dropped the piece from his mouth. Your only solicitude is to attain great riches and honors. If you believe that your interest requires you to study law or medicine, or to engage in commerce, you plunge into it at

once, without ever reflecting whether God called
you to it, or whether you can, at the same time,
attend to it and save your soul. Such scruples
as these do not even enter your head; or, if they
do, you hasten to turn to your own view the inspirations of the Holy Ghost, just as sailors
make a contrary wind serve their purpose. I
will give a specimen of the course of reasoning
generally pursued. If I become a doctor, say
you, I will get such or such a situation; when
I shall have amassed sufficient wealth, my emi-
nence will open the way to the highest prefer-
ment. If I take the ecclesiastical habit, says
another, after my theological studies, I will devote myself to the service of such a prelate; he
cannot but give me a good parish. Merchandis-
ing, says another, has often made princely for-
tunes; if I devote my resources to this, my industry will soon have doubled them; and, after
that, what may I not hope for? Such are common reasons, and would to God that those who
determine on a state of life had none worse. Is
there, in this, even the least sign of a thought
of the glory of God, the salvation of the soul,
Paradise, eternity? Where is faith? Would an
atheist, who believes neither in God nor in
eternity, reason otherwise?

But at least those who choose a religious state
have no such motives. Would to God that this

were true, for many have embraced that state, only with a hope of living more at ease. Their family is in straitened circumstances, the times are bad, they promise themselves in the cloister a more agreeable life, or an honorable office. These persons have neither vocation nor zeal: their only object is to escape misery, and live on good cheer, at the expense of Jesus Christ. A lazy tradesman, fully convinced that angels would bring his victuals to him regularly, wished on that account to become a hermit. He left his wife and little children, and retired into the woods near where another hermit dwelt, to whom he related his designs. The hour for dinner approached, came, and passed, but no angels appeared; and the man began to lose patience. "However," said he to himself, "perhaps the heavenly bread has not yet been taken from the oven." After a while he met the old hermit, and asked, "At what hour do they dine in heaven?" "What do you say," replied he, "are you crazy?" "Oh! no," said the new-comer, "I only asked, because the angel has not yet come to bring me anything to eat." "Oh! foolish man!" said the hermit, "because you have been here two hours, do you think you deserve to have angels bring you bread, as if you were one of the holy fathers of the desert? I have been living here these twenty years on raw herbs, and

8

I am not yet sure of having obtained the grace of God. You must, my brother, in order to please God, work, suffer, and eat little." "If I had wished," replied the tradesman, "to labor and eat little, I would not have left my house:" saying this, and being pressed by hunger, and in quite a bad humor, he left the forest and returned home grumbling.

Those who enter religion through temporal motives, do not generally find what they expect; and make neither good religious, nor good laymen.

CHAPTER IX.

SECTION 1. *To choose well, you must compare the perishable present with the eternal future.*

E who is susceptible of elevation of soul, of truly noble sentiments, ought not to act from base motives. Let him adopt those sentiments which have controlled the greatest men in the world. St. Ignatius wished to win to God the great soul of St. Francis Xavier, which was entirely absorbed in the pursuit of the honors which his talents promised him. "Francis," said St. Ignatius to him, "what will all you may gain in this life profit you, if you make no provision for the next? If your soul is lost for all eternity, what advantage will it be to you to have left great riches to your heirs, to have gained a celebrated name, to have led a luxurious life? would it be wise to purchase the fleeting joys of the present, at the price of eternal sufferings in the future? Do you hope to live fifty years longer? You can never be sure of that, — but let us suppose that you are certain

of it;—let us even add that you will not be
exposed to the many reverses so common to
other men, that you will reach the very pinnacle
of honor, that you will possess immense riches
and be blessed with accomplished children, and
finally, suppose that nothing will be wanting to
your temporal happiness. But what is half a
century in comparison with the endless ages of
eternity, with the punishment of hell, the happiness of heaven? Would it not be foolish to
employ a great part of life in heaping up things
which you must abandon when you die, whether
you will or not? If you employ in the service
of God, in acquiring heaven, the same, and
even less labor than the world requires, (for
which it grants a small and pitiful portion of its
despicable goods,) you will obtain fortune, honor,
and happiness, eternal and infinite." Make the
same reflections for yourself, when you choose
a state. Often recall these words, "What will
it profit me?" and thus avoid the misfortune of
crying eternally in hell with the damned, "What
hath pride profited us? or what advantage hath
the boasting of riches brought us?" (Wisdom.)

St. Philip Neri met a young knight who had
just come to Rome, to seek his fortune. The
young nobleman told him the successive grada-
tions of his hopes. At each step by which he
pretended to ascend, the Saint asked, "And after

that?" until finally the young man said, "And
after that I will die." The Saint added, "And
after death," and spoke to the young man's heart,
and made all those chimeras of the false gran-
deurs of the world in which he indulged, vanish
in a moment. He then spread before him the
infinite and eternal goods, which became from
that time the only object of his pursuit. Would
to God, we could say as much of all youths who
think of a state of life, but who are absorbed
in speculations about the great success which
awaits them. You will complete your studies
with credit, you will be honored with collegiate
degrees, elevated to posts of distinction, contract
an excellent marriage; be it so? "But after
that?" You will have your family around you;
you will acquire a considerable fortune, you will
enjoy the favor of the great, you will become a
statesman. "But after that?" Your name
will be respected in every country, the renown
of your family will continue to increase, your
children will be in high stations; grant this
also. "But what next?" You will have every
pleasure at your command, your health will be
perfect, your old age very agreeable, your life
long, very long, and very happy; I grant all.
"But after that?" Alas! after that you must
die. And after that you will have lost all, all
things temporal, all things eternal. You will
8*

have done all for time, nothing for eternity. You will have bestowed all your cares upon your welfare in this fleeting world, where, willing or unwilling, you are resting only for a moment as you pass, and you will have done little or nothing for the land in which you must dwell for all eternity.

St. Paul presents the same motive to assist us in making a good choice (Heb. xiii. 14): "We have not here a lasting city, but we seek one that is to come," we are wanderers on earth; we are journeying towards heaven. The royal prophet says, I am a stranger in the world, and on a pilgrimage to the other life; I go then as a traveller, journeying slowly, always bearing in mind the end I desire. I ought not to take the way which seems most agreeable to me, if it leads me astray, but that one which will conduct me most directly and most surely to my country.

SECTION 2. *Other maxims which should direct a choice.*

ST. AUGUSTINE has left us the maxim that directed him in the choice of a state. It is this: *Thou hast made us for thyself, O Lord, and our heart is uneasy until it rests in thee.* In God alone we find calm and repose, out of Him we experience grief and vexation. If you do not embrace the state in which you ought to

serve God, how many tribulations await you!
You hope to enjoy riches, but reverses will over-
whelm you. You think you will contract a distinguished and agreeable union, but you will
find only discord. You aspire to honors, and it
will only procure you thorns. How many things
have persons desired, which they wished to get
rid of almost as soon as they possessed them.

Every temporal good has its mixture of evil,
and it is a kind disposition of Providence, intended to detach us from temporal things. If
you choose a way through caprice, God warns
you that he will hedge it with thorns (Osee ii.),
and they shall surround you at every step.

If, on the contrary, you had taken the road to
which God called you, you would have found
peace therein. "*If thou hadst walked in the
ways of God, thou hadst surely dwelt in peace
forever.*" (Baruch iii. 13.)

Listen' to a very interesting fact, which St.
Augustine feelingly relates. John, the emperor,
was once attending the public plays at Treves,
when two of his courtiers, leaving the tumult
of the court, walked into the country, and came
across a hermit's cabin. They saw how much
this abode of peace differed from the Babylon of
the court. They found the life of St. Anthony
there, from which one of them read several
passages; but soon, transported by the love of

God, he cried out, " What do we think of gaining by so much labor and uneasiness? Can we
hope for more than to become the emperor's
favorites? But how many dangers must we
brave, to enjoy this frail happiness? What can
the emperor give us that does not cost us more
than it is worth? and whatever we get we will
perhaps keep not even during our life. But I
can·be God's friend at. once by simply wishing
it." He concluded by saying to his friend: " It
is done. I abandon all worldly hopes. I wish
to serve God. I will remain here. If you do
not wish to follow me, at least do not disturb
me ; so good-bye." " No," replied the other, " I
will not leave you, nor let you enjoy alone the
hope of so great a reward." And both began
at once to build their spiritual edifice. St.
Augustine, singularly touched by this example,
said to one of his friends, " What are we doing?
The ignorant seize the kingdom of heaven, and
we, with all our learning, risk our salvation."

Another principle equally solid and true, is to
take the state you will wish to have taken when
on your death-bed. Imagine yourself to have
reached this awful moment, when, assured that
you can live no longer, a Confessor will raise
the Crucifix, and repeat an act of contrition for
you. With the glimmering taper generally
placed near a dying person, how much better

will you see things, than in a full blaze of light
from the sun of buoyant youth? Whenever
St. Thomas was in doubt, he said to himself:
"Thomas, what will you wish to have done at
the hour of death." Imagine yourself to have
been brought before the divine tribunal, there to
be judged with the greatest exactness on all
your life, and to render an account of your talents,
graces, works done or neglected, inspirations,
affections, and thoughts: see what state you will
wish to have chosen: embrace it now, and you
have chosen well. St. Augustine assures us that
the best way of guiding ourselves is to turn to
the moment of death; because, being between
the present and the future life, we clearly see,
that temporal things there end, and eternal ones
begin. If you have not entirely lost your reason,
you will not hesitate to abandon a way which
affords but fleeting and deceitful goods, and to
take one which will lead you safely to the possession of those infinite treasures which God has
prepared for you.

Suppose, says St. Ignatius, that one of your
most intimate friends, consults you in these
terms: "I have a great desire to save my soul,
but I do not know what state I ought to choose
in order to insure success. If I remain in the
world, I will find it filled with dangers and bad
example; in it everything invites to sensual

pleasure, avarice, ambition, and, in a word, to sin. On the other hand, my health is good; I do not lack talents; I have a handsome fortune; I can succeed in an employment which pleases me; I wish to know by what road I would most surely reach a happy eternity. Tell me, as a good friend, what state I ought to choose in order to attain my end with safety." Adopt the same course for yourself which Christian wisdom would suggest to you for this friend, and your choice will be excellent.

St. Thomas exhorts you to take Jesus Christ as your adviser. Suppose then that you had had the happiness of being born when our Saviour lived in Judea, and gave men this sweet invitation: "Come to me, all ye who labor and are heavy burdened in this world, and I will give you rest." Beg of him, that, after having suffered so much for your salvation, he may be pleased to let you know the state to which he calls you. Say to him with St. Thomas: "Grant me, O Lord, the grace to know clearly what pleases thee, to desire it ardently, and accomplish it perfectly, for the glory of thy holy name. Fix my state of life, enlighten my mind, inflame my heart that I may embrace the one in which I will save myself." Then, listen to what the Lord will advise you, and perform it promptly, for it is the advice of infinite wisdom.

CHAPTER X.

SECTION 1. *No person can choose well with a bad adviser.*

T is the will of God that men should be guided by other men; even when the Holy Ghost grants us extraordinary light, he wishes us to understand that we are exposed to error, and that we should ask the advice of others, in order not to be deceived.

Solomon, the wisest of mortals, begged of God a docile heart. It was God's will that the Israelites should consult Moses. He sent Paul to Ananias, although he himself could have given his orders more promptly, having appeared to him on his way to Damascus. God often conversed with his Saints most familiarly; but in matters regarding their souls, he sent them to their Confessor. Even philosophy teaches that a man who thinks he knows and can do all things without needing any advice, is necessarily, either a God among mortals, or a beast among men. True prudence requires every one to take advice, especially in his own affairs, where passion or inclination interferes with soundness of judgment. Agamemnon, whilst very young, was called *the Wise King*, because he undertook nothing without asking, and following the advice of Nestor.

With truth, therefore, did Isocrates say to a young man: "When any one offers you advice for the direction of your affairs, examine in the first place how he takes care of his own. If he acquits himself badly, his advice will scarcely be advantageous to you. You cannot expect advice with regard to your situation, from him who evidently neglects his own. Who then can give you wise counsel for making a good choice? Your parents? friends who love you dearly? St. Thomas says, that generally we must not ask their advice, because they are often our enemies, and wish to seduce us; *Inimici hominis domestici ejus:* nobody asks advice of his enemies, and many of them conceal their enmity.

Whilst under the cloak of friendship, they picture good to us as evil; they wish to persuade us that the most favorable road to salvation is precisely that which is most advantageous to them. If by retaining us in the world, they rob us of eternal happiness: could the sworn enemy of mankind bring a greater evil

upon us? They love us, but what sort of love
is that which may prove our ruin? They love
us, but with an interested love, on account of
the temporal advantage they expect from us,
such as relief in their labors, the renown of the
family, increase of riches. They regard us as a
part of themselves; and, therefore, since a person cannot be his own adviser, they cannot be
the advisers of their children. They are interested in them, and will advise them, as if
children had no other end or aim than the profit
and pleasure of their parents.

The example of Jesus Christ proves what I
have advanced. He carried to the highest
degree his love for Mary and Joseph, and his
obedience for them; however, at the age of
twelve years, when the service of his eternal
Father was to be considered, he withdrew into
the Temple without saying a word to them
about it; and when Mary, overwhelmed with
grief because his foster-father and she "had
sought him sorrowing," complained tenderly to
him, he replied: "How is it that you sought
me? did you not know, that I must be about
my Father's business?" (Luke ii. 49.) By this
he teaches us, that in such a case it is not necessary to ask advice of our parents, but that we
may hide from them our divine inspirations, and
reply to them in the words of our divine Re-

9

deemer, should they wish to turn us aside from them.

It would be a still greater error, to ask the advice of friends and companions. This would be to imitate him who should place himself under the guidance of a blind man to be led over a dangerous pathway, at the great risk of losing his life. These worldlings are the blind ones, buried in a profound ignorance of what regards salvation, and delivered by their passion to a perverse will. They know not the simplest elements of true wisdom or virtue. *" The sensual man perceiveth not the things that are of the Spirit of God."* (1 Cor. ii. 14.) It would, therefore, be foolish to consult him upon a choice of the state of life. How many young persons would have chosen the way of salvation, had they not been led astray by friends and would-be sages? As soon as they believe that one thinks of serving God, they make a grand display of the most plausible maxims: "Take care of yourself, it is a weighty and momentous affair you are about; remember, do nothing rashly, be advised; do not undertake what you cannot carry out; you must reflect a long time, unless you wish to have cause of repentance."

Behold, says St. Bernard, a discretion that is carnal, sensual, diabolical, and inimical to salvation. St. Bernard, usually so mild, speaks here in a severe tone, because he had himself felt how powerful such advisers were, and how easily they overthrow every spiritual edifice. He had made known his vocation to his relations and friends, who made so many representations to him, that his constancy was shaken. They spoke of the good he would do in the world; assured him that his talents and amiability would lead him to the greatest honors and riches, that his constitution was too weak to endure the austerity of the cloister; that he could serve God more at his ease without flying from his acquaintances; that he would be the glory of his house and country. Young Bernard hesitated, but at last by a special grace he burst his chains, and gained the victory. He, therefore, well understands with what care we ought to conceal such inspirations; like the merchant in the Gospel, who, having found a treasure in a field, hid it, and sold all he had to buy the field, and gain that treasure. Great undertakings ought always to be kept secret to insure success.

SECTION 2. *One cannot choose badly, when well advised.*

IN order to make your choice, ask the advice of a wise man, who loves what is truly good, and knows how to discriminate the different states, and the nature of the person who desires

to make his selection. Seneca says: "All wish
to be happy, but many are deceived with regard
to the means of becoming so. One must, first
of all, take the true road, and be led to it by a
Director who knows well the end to which he
should aspire." Tobias said to his son: "Consult a wise man, that is, one who is upright,
prudent, and pious;" such a one is like him of
whom the Evangelist says: "He is a prudent
and faithful servant;" being zealous for the salvation of others, he will not deceive them, and
being enlightened by the Holy Ghost, cannot
be deceived; and as carefully as you should conceal your design from others, just so carefully,
says St. Lawrence Justinian, should you expose
it to your spiritual father. Let him know sincerely your whole interior, your sentiments, your
inclinations, your affections, your passions, your
physical strength, every thing in favor of your
design, and every thing against it; for if you
conceal any thing from him, it will be impossible
for him to guide you well.

There are some young people, who find great
difficulty in conversing with their Confessor,
and it is perhaps, because they fear that this
intercourse may bring their faults to his mind.
Unreasonable shame! says Gerson: how can
you believe that your Confessor loses esteem
and affection for you? It is very easy to see that

you have seldom made your confession, for if you had you would be convinced, that the greater the faults you disclosed to him, the more he was attached to you. Aristotle says, that to gain the love of any one, it is only necessary to reveal to him one of your most hidden secrets: and we find it true even with regard to entire strangers.—This confidence creates a truly paternal love in him in whom it is reposed. The remembrance of the fault, continues Gerson, I know not how, is entirely blotted from my mind, and I feel nothing but a tender love for the guilty one whom I have restored to innocence by regenerating him in grace; as the Apostle said, they are dear children born to grace.

St. Augustine wishes us to look upon our Confessor, not only as the judge and physician of our soul, but also as a most faithful friend, of whom the wise man says: "A faithful friend is our medicine of life," because he consoles us in our troubles, rejoices at our prosperity, and sympathizes in our adversity. He who has found such a friend, such a Confessor, has found a treasure. Let him profit by the treasure; let him go from time to time, out of confession to ask his advice, and he will always be instructed and consoled.

9 *

CHAPTER XI.

Section 1. *Practices useful for making a good choice.*

ERE God to place all men where he is pleased they should be, as he once did with Ezekiel, any solicitude on our part would be useless. But generally he invites us by a light which he infuses into our minds, and by affections which he excites in our breasts. We must, therefore, beg the Holy Ghost, the source of all knowledge, to impart to us this light and these affections, and we must also employ a pious industry in pursuit of them, for God will never draw us by force. One of the most useful means is, to withdraw for eight or ten days from all business, and retire into solitude, there to make a wise choice, regulated by the infallible maxims of the Gospel, and under the guidance of a good spiritual father. After having spent at your pleasure, and perhaps lost so many months and years, is it too much to give a few days of retreat to the making of a

good choice? You will see all things in a truer
light; you will see that up to this time you have
walked like a blind man, and have thus made
many false steps.

Consider to what state you are inclined.
Afterwards reflect on the end for which God
created you. Be careful to have a perfect indifference for all things, and esteem them, only
so far as they help you to attain your end. Beg
of God to enlighten you, and to prevent your
wandering from his Holy Will. Seek all the
reasons for and against the state you are considering; examine their true force, and how far
this state will assist you in serving God in this
life, that you may enjoy him in the life to come.
Take, with firmness, the way which seems most
advantageous under this point of view. If you
are doubtful, choose that which you will wish to
have taken at the hour of death. If it is absolutely impossible to separate yourself in retreat
from the world, take the advice which St. Bernard gave to a young man. If you wish to lend
the ear of your heart to the voice of God, sweeter
than honey, retire a little while from the cares
of the world, so that you may confidently say,
with Samuel: " Speak, Lord, Thy servant hear-
eth." And as the tumult of worldly things does
not permit his low sweet voice to reach your
ears, I advise you, whilst you, are in the bloom

of life, to take a little time every day for retiring
into a lonely church, or at least into a room where
you will not be disturbed, and where you may
withdraw your wandering thoughts from worldly
things, enter into yourself, and in the presence
of God alone, beg him to place you in the road
of salvation. You must also purify your soul
by a good confession, for the divine Wisdom will
not enter a soul sullied by sin. Sin forms between God and the sinner a cloud, which not
only intercepts the rays of the divine sun, but
also impairs the efficiency of your prayers.
*Thou hast set a cloud before thee, that our
prayer may not pass through.* (Lam. Jer. iii.)
It is requisite, also, that the soul be free from all
excess of passion, which, says Aristotle, may
disturb, and even overthrow the judgment. It
is dangerous to eat when one has a fever, because all food then serves to increase the fever,
and not the vital heart. In the same manner, it
is dangerous to deliberate during the fever of a
disordered affection, because then all arguments
tend to strengthen passion, and not reason. It
will be very useful to occupy yourself a little
while every morning, with thoughts on the
eternal truths, which ought to direct your con
duct, and to converse with your Confessor. St.
Aloysius often visited an Altar of the Blessed
Virgin, fasted on Saturday in her honor, and

frequently and devoutly received Holy Com-
munion, even at the court of Madrid. On the
Feast of the Assumption, after receiving the
Bread of Angels, he prayed that the ever blessed
Mary would obtain the assistance of the Holy
Ghost for him, and she showed him, in a most
clear and positive manner, to what state he was
called.

St. Lawrence Justinian, at the age of nineteen,
thought of making his choice, and these are his
beautiful words on this subject: "I was in the
same situation with many other young persons;
I earnestly sought peace of heart, and did not
find it in the vanity of earthly objects. One
day this desire of happiness deluged my heart.
A lady whose exterior was full of modesty and
goodness, appeared and said to me, 'Why, my
child, do you disturb yourself by seeking peace
in things which drive it from you? What you
desire depends on me, and I promise to give it
to you, if you will take me for your guide.'
Astonished, I asked this Lady who she was: I
am, replied she, the Wisdom of God, and embracing me, she filled my soul with spiritual consolation, and immediately vanished." Lawrence
felt strongly inclined to a perfect life, but, not
daring to trust his own judgment, he consulted
a friend very celebrated for his virtue. He
examined on one side the temporal goods which

he was in possession of, and those he hoped for, —nobility, riches, honors, pleasures, preferments, the prospect of a distinguished alliance by marriage, the renown of his family; on the other hand he fixed his mind on abstinence, watchings, hardships, giving up his own will, and upon all the difficulties met with in the service of God. Then, seated as a judge between these two kinds of objects, he said to himself, "Consider well what you are doing. Do you hope to be able to endure all these austerities?" At last turning his eyes to his crucified Redeemer, he said: "Thou art my hope, my strength, my refuge." Afterwards he obeyed the divine call without hesitation. He cast aside all worldly vanities, and sought true happiness in the service of God, and he found it so plentifully, that he regarded as unhappy the lot of his ancestors, who had, however, lived in splendor and luxury.

SECTION 2. *Prayer is the key that opens the treasury of divine wisdom.*

IMITATE the examples which I have just presented to you, and beg God to remove your doubts. Say with the holy king Josaphat, "Since I know not what I ought to do, I have no other resource than to lift my eyes to thee, O! Father of light;" for we should be guided in this affair by heavenly wisdom, far more than worldly wisdom; and we ought, like those who cross the sandy deserts of Arabia, to direct our course rather by the stars of heaven than by the faint footprints made by man in the sand, which every wind fills up. To obtain this wisdom, ask it humbly of God. All the Psalms are filled with suitable and fervent prayers; but especially the seven penitential Psalms, dictated more particularly by the Holy Ghost for the object which now engages us. Recite them often in your anxieties; say with the Royal Prophet: "I stretched forth my hand to thee; my soul is as earth without water; hear me speedily, O Lord; (Ps. cxlii. 6.) deign in the morning of my life to sow in my heart thy holy inspirations, for thou art my only hope. Make the way known to me wherein I should walk: (verse 8.) make me conquer the enemies of my salvation; show me thy divine will, and grant me the strength to accomplish it. I am confident that thou wilt deliver my soul from its troubles, and place me in the way to a happy eternity.

Prayer ought to precede, accompany, and follow every step you take in an affair so important. When you ask of God any thing conducive to salvation, ask it well, you are sure of obtaining it, for He has pledged his word, "*ask and you shall receive, seek and you shall find.*" Prayer is not only a sure, but also a necessary means.

St. Augustine teaches that after the first **grace,** man obtains other helps only so far as he **asks** them. Prayer is the key which opens the treasury of heavenly graces. I will repeat to you a prayer which St. Bernard addresses to the Blessed Virgin; its sentiments may inspire you to seek the aid of that powerful advocate in your perplexities and troubles. "Behold me at thy feet, O Virgin full of goodness, to obtain from thee, who art the dispenser of divine graces, that of making a good choice. No request can be more agreeable to thee than that of my knowing the will of thy divine Son; and I cannot receive a greater favor than that of being placed in the road to salvation. — Mother of good counsel, speak so clearly to my heart that all my doubts may be removed. Beautiful morning star! deliver my soul from the shades of ignorance, and in the dawn of my youth teach me the surest way of reaching heaven. It is for thee, mother of my Saviour, to be also the mother of my salvation. From whom, if not from thee, can I receive the light of the divine Sun? who will instruct me, but thou, Mother of the uncreated Wisdom? Hear then, O! Mary, my humble prayer: direct my wandering steps into the road that leads to eternal life, thou who always leadest to the good way, and from whom I can hope for true life." " *In me is all grace of the*

*way, and of the truth, in me is all hope of life
and virtue.''* (Eccl. xxiv.)

SECTION 3. *It is useful to read the lives of those
who have chosen well.*

IT has often occurred that excellent fruits have
been produced by reading the lives of the Saints,
even when taken up, only to relieve some tedious
moment, and for the want of amusing books.—
When you consider the actions of the Saints,
grace moves you to ask: What hinders me from
imitating them, at least in part? They had the
same nature that I have, the same inclinations,
the same temptations; still, they became chaste
and humble, despised greatness and riches.
Worldlings suffer for the world, Saints for God.
What hinders me from walking in their footsteps? Such reflections give birth to the noblest
resolutions.

St. Theresa, when a child, frequently read the
lives of the Saints. The examples of an Agnes
of thirteen years, rejoicing in the flames of martyrdom, — an Euphrasina, entering a cloister in
the bloom of youth, — a Catharine, hardly more
than a prattling child, practising the most difficult virtues, inflamed her so strongly with divine
love that she resolved to imitate them, and
actually left home to seek martyrdom among the
Infidels in Africa: but, being brought back, she

10

tried to imitate the holy Anchorets, by building
a cell in her garden, where she frequently retired
to pray and do penance. Thus, she made up for
her disappointment by living retired from the
world, and by devoting all her time to the culti-
vation of those virtues which afterwards exalted
her to so high a degree of perfection. This
reading offers the sweetest attractions, and
singularly urges us to follow the examples we
most admire.

SECTION 4. *Power of the example of others:
good inspirations resulting therefrom.*

THERE are some very interesting events con-
nected with the vocation of Father Angelus of
Joyeuse, a French Duke, who acquired considerable distinction in the history of his country.—
Being, from his youth, especially inspired to quit
the world, he found no repose until he joined
the order of Capuchins, in which he made rapid
strides towards religious perfection.

The public good afterwards required that, having a dispensation from the Sovereign Pontiff,
he should resume the command of armies, and
he thus found himself in situations as difficult
as perilous. He soon lost his love for purity,
and became so enamored of arms that he cared
to read only of feats of chivalry. But Providence gave him an opportunity to read the life

of St. Francis Borgia, then newly published — and it made such an impression upon his mind that he immediately abandoned all, and returned to the Capuchins.

If, after having employed all these means, you are still in doubt; if you are one of those of whom the Prophet says (Ps. ii. 6), " They say; who sheweth us good things," you will find a reply in the following verse: " *The light of thy countenance, O Lord! is signed upon us.*" Our minds are illumined with the light of God's countenance, — the light of reason as men, and that of Faith as Christians. These lights shine brilliantly before our eyes, and we surely shut them with obstinacy if we do not see. No subtle speculations are necessary, no long studies, or intense application of the mind, to find your vocation. It is a favor infallibly promised to him, who seeks it with attention, and with a pure and upright heart.

It must, however, be remarked, that you ought not to expect of the Holy Ghost, a light of in-contestable evidence ; nor affections so strong as to draw the will almost by force. For, generally, it is enough, if you judge from reasonable motives, and with convincing proof, that this or that state is the best for you, and the only one that will insure your eternal welfare. This kind of choice is even more sure, and more approved by masters of a spiritual life, than that which proceeds only from the sensible motion of the will. Therefore, examine the *pro* and the *con*, with regard to the end for which you are created, and conclude by choosing that one which will be the surest to lead you to salvation.

As for my part, I do not fear that God will not speak to your heart; but I do fear, that you will not hear his voice. No pains are necessary, says St. Bernard, in order to hear the voice of God; but some are necessary, if you wish to shut your heart lest it may enter. This divine voice presents itself to us, asks to be admitted, and never ceases knocking at the door of our hearts. You yourself will have perceived, in reading these reflections, *some ray* of light; you will have felt one or another invitation, and perhaps you have closed the book, because you were afraid some divine inspiration might take root in your heart.

CHAPTER XII.

SECTION 1. *Those ungrateful persons who obsti-
nately resist the call of God, are in the end
deprived of his graces.*

THE Lord never refuses his light, but
how many shut their eyes that they
may not see it! They resemble a
man who closed his windows to keep
the light out, so that he would have
no reason to thank God for making the sun
shine.—Do such persons think that God will call
them to a less strict account for the light he had
offered them, because they close the windows of
their hearts to avoid receiving it? God calls
them by the most tender words of the best of
fathers; but they have not been moved, because
they are firmly fixed to the earth. God gives
them inspirations, but they fall on a rock: He
sends them chastisements, but they do not startle
them: He pours his graces on them, but they
harden like clay beneath the sun: He shows
them an eternity of happiness, or of misery, but

the former does not attract, nor the latter frighten
them.—What then will happen to these obstinate hearts? God will withdraw his help from
them; that is, he will not, for the future, offer
them certain gifts which we have not deserved,
and which he has not promised us, but with
which He enriches, through pure liberality,
whomsoever he pleases. —Although God offers
every person sufficient aid to enable him to save
himself; still, he does not give every person
that abundant aid which would enable him to
easily conquer all difficulties, and he generally
refuses extraordinary helps to the obstinate.

God grants graces, says the Scripture, "with
weight and measure." On our correspondence
to a certain number of graces, or our refusal of
them, depends our salvation, or our loss. "Jerusalem! Jerusalem! how many times have I
wished, by my graces, to convert thy inhabitants,
and gather them in my arms as the hen gathereth
her little ones under her wings, and thou wouldst
not!—In punishment of thy obstinacy, I will
abandon thee to thy enemies; thou shalt be the
victim of my indignation." "*How many times?*"
behold the graces are counted, which have been
granted to save you! "*But thou wouldst not:*"
behold the refusal the soul makes! "*I will
abandon thee:*" behold thy reprobation and loss.
Jericho refused to open her gates to the people

of God; Joshua, according to the order he had received, marched around the city seven times, sounding the trumpet. The inhabitants did not surrender at the first six notices; at the seventh, the walls fell, and all perished by fire and sword. Such is the picture of an obstinate soul which God has decreed to call a certain number of times, and no more. If the soul does not make use of these graces whilst she can, when she is deprived of all, whom ought she to blame but herself? It is with justice that God withdraws his blessings from those who abuse his goodness. Weigh well these reflections, and say to yourself: who knows if this call is not the last I am to receive from heaven.

SECTION 2. *Terrible punishments inflicted on those who do not obey God.*

LET us consider the connection which God has established between the punishment and the fault of those who do not obey. When a ray of inspiration appears, they shut their eyes. The punishment in this case, is a blindness with regard to Heaven and the importance of salvation. They have been rebels to light, says Job; they have not wished to take the road which God showed them; they will be in darkness, and think themselves in the midst of bright-

ness.   Hear what Moses says to those unhappy
wanderers.   The Lord will strike you with
blindness and madness, and you will grope in
the midst of heavenly light, as the blind man is
wont to grope in the dark, and you will no
longer know how to take the good way.   Behold
what such a soul comes to!   The punishment is
proportioned to the fault, says St. Augustine:
she loses the help of which she did not make a
good use when it was in her power to do so.
Inspiration is the voice of God.   When a person
closes his ears to avoid hearing it, he is punished
with hardness of heart; he no longer cares for
divine promises, or divine threats, and says with
the impious Pharaoh, — " Who is he, whose
voice, you say, I ought to hear and whose orders
execute?   I know no other gods than the idols
of my thoughts and affections."   He concludes
by imitating the asp, which places one ear
against the ground, and stops the other with its
tail, to avoid hearing the songs of those who
would calm its ferocity.   In the same manner a
soul has no longer any thoughts of heaven:
glued to the earth, she no longer hears the
thunders of divine justice ; she falls asleep in
the midst of God's threats. (Ps. iv. 7.)   What
a misfortune, says St. Augustine, to be lulled to
sleep by the same sounds that awaken others.
This is the frightful punishment of those who

are accustomed to neglect the warnings of God
Inspiration is a movement of the heart, which
excites the will. The punishment of those who
neglect it, is often a hardness of heart, which
makes the soul so insensible, that she is no
longer susceptible of any good impression. If
God wishes to purify her by afflictions, and
assaults her with his chastisements, she shuts
herself up in the fortress of her obstinacy, and
no longer feels her misfortunes, as she confesses
by the mouth of the wise man, "They have
struck me, but I have not even perceived it."
If, on the contrary, God wishes to gain such a
soul by favors, nothing affects her; she becomes
even more hardened. "At thy rebuke, O God
of Jacob, they have all slumbered." Her state
is deplorable: neither promises of Heaven, nor
calamities of earth, nor instructions, nor examples
are capable of raising her thoughts above the
world. She becomes, says the prophet, like a
carcass, feeling a cut with a knife no more than
the touch of a straw, and seeing no better by
the light of the sun than by the glimmer of a
spark.

God says by his prophet Osee, Woe to them,
for they have departed from me: behold the
fault. Woe to them, when I shall be far from
them: behold the consequence. Woe to them
when I shall have abandoned them to their

blindness, to their deafness, to the hardness of their hearts. At the close of this work, I will mention some examples of these hardened souls. I will now present the different states which may be the object of a choice.

CHAPTER XIII

SECTION 1. *An exact idea of the Secular State.*

IT is evident that cloisters, where so many examples of virtue are found, are the beaten path to heaven. It is also very true, as St. Jerome says (Ep. 15), that in all states there is a way to heaven, marked by the footsteps of some great Servants of God. I will only present you with some short reflections on the different states, without leading you towards any one, so that having considered all, you may choose the one best calculated to insure the salvation of your soul.

I begin with the secular state. Who will deny that we find in it great opportunities of laying up treasures for eternal life? why may we not enjoy our property, and relieve the poor? live independently, and observe the commandments of God? acquire riches, honors, friends, and be strictly just? What treasures of merit cannot those seculars acquire, who, like Tobias, teach their children to fear God, and abstain from all sin! A zealous Christian can maintain piety in his family, assist the poor by alms, and incite his fellow-creatures to virtue by his good example. There are some in all states who practise heroic virtues, and merit an immense reward in heaven.

We certainly see some merchants, not only faithful to the laws of justice, but also eager, by their liberal alms, to lay up treasures in heaven There are lawyers and magistrates, who, like St. Ivo, perfectly fulfil their duties, and support the rights of the poor; courtiers in the midst of honors, who, like St. Eleazar, only set their hearts on the great things of heaven. Is there a religious with a purer heart than St. Louis, king of France? a Priest with more lively faith than St. Maurice, commander of a legion? St. Anthony of Padua was very much surprised when he learned from God, that a certain city clerk would be higher in heaven than he. In a word, then, every state may lead us to heaven.

But let us turn the picture, and we will see that in the secular state there is great danger of losing the soul. Philosophers enumerate eleven evil passions born with man, and which, even without exterior causes, keep up a continual warfare within. Ambition, Luxury, Envy, Anger, and their evil consequences, excite such furious tempests within us, as to expose us to constant danger of destruction. But when to our bad interior inclinations, the world adds occasions and stimulants, everywhere to be met with,— when it offers insult to anger, ease to idleness, threats to fear, persecutions to envy, incitements to pride, delicate dishes to gluttony, riches to avarice, disasters to despair, reproach to shame, and to luxury, indelicate conversations, parties, plays, and friendships full of danger,—and when it does all it can do for each passion and each vice, by supplying everything that can nourish and excite it,—what will be the result? Reflect upon the snares, the evil company, licentious conversation, and perverting maxims of the world, and you will say with the Prophet Osee, "I see a deluge of wickedness, of slander, of falsehood, of murder, of robbery, of impurities:" and with St. John, "The whole world swims in iniquity." Is it then easy to escape? seeing that wherever you plant your foot there are thorns, and that by escaping one trap you fall into another. You walk in the midst of snares, says the Wise man, in the midst of ambushes in riches, in pleasures, and in intercourse with the world.

St. Anthony saw the whole world covered with snares, set by pride, avarice, luxury, and more than all, by the Devil who is eagerly seeking to destroy our souls. Who will not be

11

caught sooner or later? St. Ambrose, who knew all the states of the world by experience, says, in his admirable book, *De Fugá Sæculi*, that its ways are like the streets of Babylon, and seculars walk in the midst of a perverse nation. Who can save himself in roads beset by assassins? St. Jerome, retiring from the world into the solitude of Bethlehem, cries out to youth: Take great care of yourselves, for in the world, the Devil in his fury turns to all sides, lies in ambush to take souls, and all hell is armed against you. See, above all, the pleasures which decoy you into danger; avarice contriving fraud, ambition lying in wait, and bad companions like syrens enticing you. The sovereign remedy, therefore, is flight.

It is however true, that God is pleased to show examples of virtue in the world, that are more wonderful than those amongst religious; but these are very rare favors; it would often be rashness to hope for them; for generally, he who lives in danger perishes therein. It is a continual wonder, says Plato, for a man to have vice in his power, and virtue in his will; that a man in the midst of a thousand dangers could do all he wishes, and never wish what is unlawful. It is also a great wonder to be amid licentious entertainments without sinning, to deal continually in money without contracting avarice, to suffer insults without resenting them, to live amid honors without ambition, except through Him by whose power Daniel remained untouched amongst lions, and Agnes in the midst of flames without a single hair being burned.

SECTION 2. *Other remarks on the Secular State.*

A PARTISAN of the world will perhaps say, that there are preservatives against falling, and remedies in case one does fall; that he can frequent the sacraments; that he does not lack spiritual aid; masses, offices, sermons, festivals, which foster piety. Why cannot a good secular go to communion every month? occasionally read books on eternal truths? converse with his spiritual Father on the interests of his soul? why can he not imitate Isaac who went to meditate in the fields? what will hinder his following also the example of holy King David, who, though governing a kingdom, found time to raise his mind to God seven times a day? A person must not necessarily be too eager of gain, or burden himself with the affairs of the world until his mind is overpowered by them. It is sufficient, according to the advice of the Wise man, to be economical of time, to divide it between temporal affairs and heavenly interests.

It would be difficult to prove that the world is less dangerous now than in former times. Mer-

chants will tell you, that commerce is now so
intricate, that none can succeed in it but the art-
ful and crafty.   Lawyers will tell you, that virtue and science have almost no influence, for
offices are given to the highest bidder, and consequently it is very difficult for those who fill
them to hold the scales of justice aright.   It is
true that in the world there are many spiritual
aids ; and it is likewise very true, that seculars
make very little use of them.   Meditation is a
word of which very few know the meaning.   It
is a great deal if young gentlemen, just out of
their studies, approach the sacraments three or
four times a year.   They do listen to sermons, it
is true ; but is it to profit by them ?   Do they
not sneer at those who are virtuous and pious,
and call them the would-be reformers of the
world ?   Temporal misfortunes deprive a man
of every spiritual thought ; he loses some of his
property, is stripped of some paltry dignity, or
is impoverished by law-suits ; a wife seldom
fails to cause great vexation ; vicious children,
gamesters, and libertines, impose continual care
and anxiety upon him ; his property is wasted
by faithless servants.   What sighs !   What dis-
appointments !   Is it in the midst of such turmoils and troubles as these that he hopes to find
time for thinking of his soul ?

But, lest you should imagine that I wish .to

entice you out of the world, I will cite a very
interesting example for seculars. St. Paphnucius,
after having lived in great perfection in the
desert for fifty years, had the curiosity to ask
God, if any one served Him as he did. God
pointed out. to him a drummer, in Alexandria,
whose perfection resembled that of Paphnucius.
The latter hastened to seek the drummer, and
having found him, urged him to relate his course
of conduct.   The drummer frankly confessed
that he had been an assassin, but had saved the
honor of some ladies, that he divided amongst
the poor the small salary which he received as
drummer, and finally, said he, "I love God and
the poor; this is what I do."   Paphnucius,
astonished that a secular was so perfect, returned
in confusion to the desert, and applied himself
more earnestly to perfection.   But soon he was
so curious as to ask again of God, whom he
resembled.   The angel replied that in a neigh-
boring village there was a Count whose virtue
was of the same degree as his.   The solitary,
not understanding how a courtier could equal a
hermit in virtue, immediately repaired to the
village.   As soon as he appeared at the castle,
the Count wished to wash his feet, and seat him
at table.   But Paphnucius declared that, having
learned from an angel that many monks were
inferior to him in virtue, he would accept of
11*

nothing until the Count had told his manner of
life. The latter, much confused, felt obliged to
say: "1st. I entertain all travellers who go this
way. 2d. I give alms to the poor. 3d. I believe
I possess nothing that belongs to others. 4th.
I always give my first thoughts to God, and am
not attached to any object of this world." The
saint, bursting into tears, embraced the Count
affectionately, and said to him: I have lived
fifty years in the desert, to purify my heart, and
my soul is not yet so pure, nor my heart so
full of God as your's. Would you believe it?
Paphnucius, having exercised himself in religious
virtues more earnestly for a while, asked a third
time of God, whom he resembled. The angel
replied to him: you resemble a jeweller who is
passing by your door. How! said Paphnucius,
will I always be sent to drummers, courtiers,
merchants: to these people who are deluged
with temporal occupations, and rarely have time
to think of God? However, having found the
merchant, he so pressed him as to draw from
him this reply: "I firmly believe, that I have
nothing to do in this world, but to gain heaven.
I travel over land and sea, firmly persuaded that
all my labors should tend towards heaven.
With what I gain I help the poor, in order that
they may be my advocates. I desire only eternal
life." Great God! exclaimed the anchoret, who

would ever have believed that there was so much purity in the heart of a merchant? He returned to the desert, and was very much humbled to find so much holiness among seculars. I have shown you the advantages of a secular life; but I ought in conscience to warn you, that such examples as I have just related, are very rare in the world. Divine Providence has given, in every state, some great model, in order that those of the same state may not despair; but these are very few, and we therefore have no right to presume. We must apply to this subject, the reflection of St. Augustine upon the good thief; it is this: *Unus ne desperes, solus ne præsumas. There is one, do not despair; there is only one, do not presume.* We meet in the world a hundred times more occasions of losing our souls than of saving them. It is *Jesus Christ* himself, who says, that it is very difficult for the rich to be saved; that it is easier for a camel to pass through the eye of a needle, than for a rich man to enter the kingdom of Heaven. St. Chrysostom, addressing from the pulpit a crowd of five thousand, exclaimed: "Think you that out of this great number, one hundred will be saved?"

Oh! how many people of the world, in all states of life, cry out at the hour of death: "Would to God I had never been burdened with temporal affairs." Leo XI. said, when at the point of death, "How much better it would have been for me to have held the keys of my monastery gate, than those of Heaven!"

Remember, lastly, that the wise and virtuous Sir Thomas More used to say, "*This world is so void of gratitude, that it will not reward good actions; and is so poor, that even if it wished it could not.*"

CHAPTER XIV.

SECTION 1. *An accurate view of the Clerical State.*

HE life of a secular Priest enjoys neither the solitude of the cloister nor the liberty of the world. It seems to hold a middle place between them, and is consequently better adapted to the nature of man. Its duties are directed to God, and consist in studying the Scriptures, teaching Christian doctrine, reciting the divine office—which contains the most pious sentiments, and celebrating Mass — from which so much fruit is drawn. In fine, the Apostle defines the Secular Priest, when he says: "Free from worldly ties, he thinks of the things of God." But these words cannot be applied to all ecclesiastics. They do not suit such as are engrossed with temporal affairs, whether of their family or of the public, who give themselves up to the management of property, or distracting business of any kind, the care of their nephews, and a thousand other engagements which over-

power the mind, and consume the time that
should be spent in spiritual exercises. St.
Gregory, after having quoted the text of Jeremiah on this subject: "How is the gold become
dim, the finest color is changed, the stones of
the sanctuary are scattered in the top of every
street," adds in addressing Priests: "We are
the stones of the sanctuary, who should never
be seen employed in works foreign to our high
calling, — but now, there is hardly any secular
affair that is not administered by Priests."

This deplorable evil is often followed by
another still greater. Instead of employing the
ecclesiastical revenues to the advantage of the
Church, they employ them in enriching their
family. They are not good pastors, but bad
merchants. How many young people take the
tonsure, only because they have a rich and
honored uncle among the Clergy.

"There are some amongst the Clergy," says
St. Jerome, "who, whilst serving our poor
Christ, possess riches which they would not
have obtained by remaining in the world: so
that the Church sighs over these rich men,
whom the world once regarded as beggars."
(Ep. 2.) Perhaps these persons had not intentions quite so bad when they received Holy
Orders, but by degrees, as they obtained property, they yielded to these sentiments, and are

now more engaged with temporal affairs than seculars.

The Holy Canons teach, that ecclesiastics have no right to employ at their caprice, the goods which are the patrimony of Jesus Christ, the Church, and the poor. The Priest can use them for his honest support, but not to contribute to luxury and vanity, nor to benefit or gratify his relations.

The common sentiment of the Doctors of the Church is, that having what suits his state, the remainder must go to the poor, and to ornament churches. He will have to render an exact account of it on the day of judgment.

When persons enter Holy Orders through motives so base, what terror should not strike them as they read this positive sentence of St. Bernard: "If persons, through a desire of worldly gain, make piety a matter of money, their damnation is certain."

St. Charles Borromeo, at the age of fifteen, when a large Church income fell to him by the demise of his uncle, declared to his father, that the revenues of this benefice could not be applied to the benefit of his family, because they were the patrimony of Jesus Christ, and he was not the owner, but the administrator: he wished, therefore, that the revenues of the patrimonial goods should be accounted for, and that the poor should receive their portion. St. Charles did not think this use of goods to be only a simple act of perfection, but a strict obligation; and he often declared it to his clergy. St. Exuperius, Bishop of Toulouse, says: "There is the same difference between a layman robbing the church, and an ecclesiastic squandering church revenues, as between a highway robber, and a servant robbing his master of goods entrusted to his care. The one uses force, the other fraud."

This Saint stripped his palace to adorn the Church, and in time of need stripped the Church to relieve the poor. Those persons, then, commit a great crime who expend the patrimony of Jesus Christ for the benefit of their relations, and not for that of the poor.

SECTION 2. *Other reflections on the Ecclesiastical State.*

WE ought to say the same of the Ecclesiastical state, as of the voyage to the Indies: *magna merces, sed majus periculum: Great profit, but greater peril.* No doubt, by daily offering the Holy Sacrifice of the Mass, we can lay up great treasures in Heaven, and acquire strength to live free from mortal sin; for the Holy Council of Trent says, that this Sacrament is an antidote which frees us from venial faults, and preserves us from those that are mortal.

St. Philip Neri assures us, that if a Priest celebrates mass well, it is sufficient to enable him to preserve his holy affections the rest of the day : and Orsini declares, that nothing is more powerful in aiding him to resist temptations ; for if he meets them in the morning, he chases them away with the thought that he is soon to receive Jesus Christ; if in the evening, by reflecting that he is to communicate next morning. All this is very true ; still I repeat, " great profit, but greater peril." The Holy Sacrifice is a rich mine of graces, but, to draw them out, a person must have a large capital of virtue : he must lead a very pure life, but it is difficult to do this amid the dangers which the world presents. St. Francis of Assisium having learned from an Angel what should be the purity of a Priest, never dared to become one. St. Chrysostom says, that "a Priest should be purer than the sun." As the sun's rays fall in the mire and amongst poisonous herbs, without being soiled by the one or poisoned by the other, so should a Priest walk amid the innumerable vices that deluge the world, and not be tainted. His mind should be as incorruptible as the bodies of the three youths in the Babylonian furnace. As they stood untouched amid flames, so should a Priest preserve every virtue amid the flames of worldly vices, luxury, ambition, and interest.

Finally, a Priest is often obliged to see dangerous objects, to hear in confession revolting accusations, and still, like Lot, he must preserve the purity of his sight and hearing. But where is the man that can do this?

It is hard, very hard, to live in the midst of so many risks of every kind, the attacks of so many enemies, snares so multiplied, without losing that integrity of conscience to which he is obliged who consecrates and administers the sacraments. Hear St. Chrysostom. "I do not speak lightly," says he, "but as I think; I really believe there are not many in the Priesthood who save their souls, but very many who are lost:" and their damnation is so much the more certain, as they have committed greater faults by abusing invaluable blessings. It is true, that Priests in a religious order are exposed to many inconveniences; but it is evident, that in their cloisters they have fewer dangers and more helps than secular Priests, of whom it may be said, that they have almost the same obligations that regular clergy have, and are beset by the same dangers as worldlings.

Consider now, another great privilege granted to Priests, that of helping to save souls: "We are helpers of God." They co-operate with God for the salvation of souls; is there a greater dignity? They are the dispensers of divine favors in the sacraments; can a person procure a greater glory for God? Is there a treasury from which we can draw more merits? St. Dennis says: "Among divine things, the most divine is to co-operate with God, for the salvation of man." And St. Chrysostom: "Though you should distribute immense wealth to the poor, you do more by converting a single soul." A good Priest can therefore lay up incalculable merits, by nourishing souls with the word of God, by absolving their sins in the tribunal of penance, and by dispensing grace in the sacrament of the Eucharist. "But," says St. Bernard, "since the office of saving souls is entirely divine, it ought to frighten those who are obliged to it, such as parish Priests." It is a burden to be dreaded even by angels. SS. Gregory, Ambrose, and Chrysostom, understood this so well, that they fled when the Church wished· to impose upon them the care of souls; and St. Nilamon died through fear of it. It is very difficult to answer for our own souls; how much more so to account for those of others! The Scripture says: "*A most severe judgment shall be for them that bear rule.*" Priests administer the sacraments; but this may be for

them an occasion of sacrilege. In becoming
useful to those whose confessions they hear,
they often hurt themselves; like the file, which,
in cleansing iron, soils and injures itself. Priests
glorify God in saving souls; but if they lose
their own souls by negligence, they waste a
treasure purchased with the life of God. Obliged
to prevent scandal when they can, it may happen
that the fear of irritating a great man, or of
displeasing a friend, will prevent their condemn-
ing it. They are the light of the world; but if
they have worldly ways, they dishonor the
Church. God receives no greater insult, says
St. Gregory, than from Priests, when he sees
that those whom he has put to save others, are
an example of wickedness to them. Or if they
be dumb when they should speak, silent where
they should raise their voices, they are like the
Heathen Idols, and woe to them! "Woe to the
pastors of Israel, who feed themselves and starve
their flocks."

Such is the state of a secular Priest; there
is none that requires a life so pure, and which
at the same time offers more occasions of sin.
I do not seek to withdraw you from it, if God
calls you to it, but I show you its dangers, in
order that you may undertake it only from
supernatural motives. Its dignity surpasses all
the grandeur of earth, even that of Monarchs;

it is, indeed, above that of Angels, both on account of the power of consecrating the Body of our Lord, and that of remitting sins, — privileges so sublime, that if the Mother of God were here on earth, she could not exercise them. A Priest's life must therefore correspond to his dignity; his heart must be entirely united to God, his exterior entirely different from that of other people, giving a just idea of his holiness: "Let thy priests be clothed in justice," says the royal Psalmist. If a Priest thinks of evil, it is a sin; if he commits it, a sacrilege, and if he carries it to the Altar, it is an enormous crime. How pure must those lips be, which receive the Son of God! How clean those hands, chosen to loose souls from the bonds of sin! How chaste the heart, watered with the blood of the Word made flesh! If God calls you, obey his voice, but strive to increase the number of those who have honored this state by their great holiness and admirable learning

12*

CHAPTER XV.

SECTION 1. *True picture of the Religious State.*

 WILL borrow the words of St. Bernard, who has given an excellent description of the religious state. In a sermon on the text: *The kingdom of heaven is like unto a merchant who seeks pearls, and having found a precious one, he sells all he has to buy it.* The Saint says, that the precious pearl is *the religious life, where man lives more purely, falls more rarely, rises more quickly, advances more securely in the path to perfection, is refreshed more frequently with heavenly grace, reposes more tranquilly, dies with more confidence, is purified more quickly, and rewarded more abundantly.* Let us examine these advantages.

The Religious "lives more purely, and falls more rarely," because he is far away from the snares met in the world at every step. The sources of sin, says St. John, comprise all that is in the world, "concupiscence of the flesh, concupiscence of the eyes, and pride of life."

138

The love of sensual pleasure generally depraves youth. The desire of wealth, says the Apostle, is the root of all evil; ambition is the source of a crowd of vices; and the desire of liberty engages us to satisfy passions, which, once let loose, know no bounds. Bad example, human respect, and corrupt manners are terrible occasions of falls, and it is easily seen that these dangers are entirely escaped, or at least very much diminished in a religious life. By the vow of chastity, a religious renounces the love of sensual pleasures; by that of poverty, the desire of property; by that of obedience, his own will. The Wise man says on the subject of sensuality, that it is incomparably easier to abstain entirely from unwholesome fruits, than to eat temperately of them, when we have once tried their sweetness. Moreover, he who does not dwell in an abode of pleasures, riches, and honors, is less moved to desire them. The very retirement of the cloister forbids loose discourse and scandalous manners. Add to this advantage the twelve helps which Lessius enumerates in a religious life: the rules of the institute, the light of prayer, meditation on eternal things, reading the Holy Scriptures, examinations of conscience, the direction of superiors, good example, frequenting the Sacraments, mortification of the appetite, good distribution of time, ex-

ercises of every virtue and the particular care
of the Holy angels. With such helps it is evident, that the religious "lives more purely and
falls more rarely." This is why St. Mary Mag-
dalen, of Pazzi, would often in a rapture cling
to the walls of the monastery and kiss them,
exclaiming: " Oh! lovely walls, from how many
dangers ye preserve me." At other times she
said: " If persons knew what safety and happiness are found in the service of God, they would
scale the walls of monasteries to obtain a place
in them."

If through weakness a religious sometimes
falls, *he rises more quickly*, for the same reasons
that he falls more rarely. St. Thomas adds,
that a fallen religious is helped by his brothers
to rise immediately, as the Holy Ghost teaches:
" he will be helped by another," by his companions, whose good example he will have, or by
the advice of his superior. It is often enough
for him to disclose his temptation to his spiritual father — who is always at hand — and it
immediately vanishes; either on account of the
humiliation of declaring his miseries and sub-
mitting to another, or because the Devil, seeing
his snares exposed, loses the boldness he as-
sumed when fighting in secret. Moreover, the
abundant graces of religion effectually deliver
him from the abyss of sin, or, as Origen explains

it, "When the religious falls, his fall is not followed by his ruin; because the Lord places his merciful hand under him to lift him up." Jesus Christ himself declared to St. Catharine, that religion is not a steep but a level road; and he who falls therein does not fall down a precipice, but remains where he has fallen, and receives strength to rise.

Another privilege is that of *advancing more securely in the path to perfection;* because he obtains more light to know his dangers, or that his superiors guard him, or finally, the remembrance of his vows brings to mind the obligation he has contracted. But one of the greatest helps he has in religion for avoiding even little falls, is to arrest the first movement towards great ones; for in combating small defects, he either conquers or falls; if he falls, it is but a small hurt; if he conquers, he acquires the art of conquering, and becomes more capable of defeating the Devil in more serious contests.

The fifth privilege consists in being *oftener refreshed with heavenly grace.* The religious receives more frequently the dew of Heaven, the light of the divine Sun, and the consolations of the Holy Ghost. These advantages are less common in the world. The secular, tossed to and fro by passions, does not even understand what the peace of a good conscience is; his palate, depraved by sensual delights, knows not the taste of the honey of heavenly consolations. If now and then worldlings experience these joys after a good confession, we hear them say, that their contentment surpasses all the pleasures of the world. When they worthily approach the Sacraments, and give some time to prayer, they avow, that they find therein a peace, a happiness, which they would seek in vain in any thing else. Religious who have renounced the pleasures of the world, obtain delights in the greatest abundance, and would not exchange a single day of their felicity, for an age of those pleasures which those happy ones of the world so much extol. It is the same with them as with St. Francis Xavier, and St. Ephraim, who begged God to moderate the consolations He poured into their bosoms, for their hearts were too feeble to endure that excess of joy.

The religious enjoys more tranquillity, because his repose is beyond the reach of disturbance, and he is removed from the storms and dangers of the world. St. Bernard says, explaining the words of the canticle of Solomon, "Our bed is flourishing;" "I think that the beds of the beloved in our Church are the monasteries, in which the religious live quietly, and are free

from the solicitudes of the world." But whence
is this tranquillity? The affections being moderate, the religious feels lightly, what would wound
a secular severely: besides, his hope of eternal
happiness is a never-failing fountain of joy. To
understand the peace of a religious, it is only
necessary to cast a glance at the troubles that
disturb seculars. But as people nearer the pole
do not well understand the disadvantages of
their cold climate until they enjoy for a while
our more temperate region, so you cannot justly
estimate the enormous burden which the world
imposes upon its followers, till you have experienced the lightness of the yoke of Jesus
Christ. The Emperor Theodosius left the Court
one day, alone and disguised, to visit the cell of
a hermit, and rest a little while from the anxieties
attached to the throne. He perceived in a bag
a little piece of bread, and asked the religious
for some of it. They sat down and ate together;
but with what relish! what tranquillity! Theodosius said to the religious: "My father, do
you know who I am?" "How can I know, for
I never leave this place?" "Know that I am
the Emperor Theodosius." The religious hastened to pay him some mark of respect. "Sit
down," said the Emperor, "and remember, that
if there is any happiness on earth, it is for religious, far away from the vexations of the

world. I assure you from experience, that amidst the delights of my court, I never take food without finding in it more wormwood than honey." Thus this wise Prince considered happy, not the great of the world, but the poor servants of God, occupied only with gaining Paradise, of which they receive a foretaste even in this valley of tears.

SECTION 2. *Other privileges of the Religious State.*

ALTHOUGH the advantages already spoken of would be valued as nothing, there is another that is inestimable. The religious *dies with more confidence.* He is not subjected to the grief of leaving his possessions, to uneasiness for sins committed, to the fear of possessing ill-gotten wealth, to the trouble of making a good will. He recalls his faults, but has every reason to hope for pardon. St. Chrysostom says on this subject: " Religious also die, but what is their death? It offers nothing frightful. They accompany it with holy canticles, and it seems to spectators rather a triumph than a struggle. The religious who witnessed the last moments of the departed, rejoice at his happiness, envy his lot, and earnestly desire to enter with him into eternal rest. The religious sees no wife bathed in tears, no lonely children uneasy about their future conditions. He only thinks that his death ought to be worthy of a man who has lived but to please God, and is now going to enjoy him for all eternity. He seems to hear Jesus say: 'Come, ye blessed of my Father, possess the Kingdom prepared for you. You have observed obedience; it is then for your Superior, rather than for yourself, to render an account of your life; for it is not the soldier, who is accountable for his deeds, but the general who commands him.'"

The pious and learned Suarez said, in his last moments: "My God, how lovely is death! how sweet it is! Ah! since it is so sweet to die united to God, what will it not be to live with him eternally. I would never have believed that one could taste so much pleasure in death, although I had often called the death of a religious, a sleep to which succeeds eternal glory." *When he shall give sleep to his beloved, behold the inheritance of the Lord.* Gerard, the brother of St. Bernard, had spent at Clairvaux a perfectly religious life. When he was told of his approaching end, he was filled with so great a consolation, that he chanted the Psalm *Laudate Dominum de cælis.* St. Bernard, who was present with the other religious, pictures to us the feelings he experienced at this kind of a miracle. "What a wonder to see a man overwhelmed

13

with joy at the moment of death. O death! where is thy victory? the dying man sings! Death, elsewhere a source of sadness, is here a source of joy! Gerard goes to meet it, not only with confidence, but with gladness! Happy those who, already dead to the world, die in the Lord; the Holy Ghost invites them to rest from their labors, for their good works will follow them."

The religious is *purified more quickly* in Purgatory, either because the guilt and punishment of sins committed in the world are remitted when he embraces a religious life, says St. Thomas, or because he has satisfied in great part during his life, or finally, because his brothers offer masses and good works for him.

The religious is *rewarded more abundantly*, for he practises in his cloister a multitude of virtues; such as charity, patience, poverty, mortification, humility, and temperance, and he makes acts of these virtues almost every moment; but these acts are more meritorious, because they are commanded by the rules; more precious, because he is obliged thereto by vows so agreeable to God, and are therefore more precious than the same virtues practised in the world through a person's own free choice. Add to these interior acts the many holy exterior occupations; such as preaching, hearing confessions, catechizing, giving good advice, visiting the sick, converting sinners,—occupations so common to religious. It is by these that they merit the reward promised in the Gospel of St. Matthew: *He that shall do and teach, he shall be called great in the kingdom of heaven*, (v. 19.) You may read on this subject the admirable little work of Father Nieremberg, in which he proves, that by obedience alone a religious sanctifies the lowest and most indifferent actions, such as eating, working, and sleeping, when in performing them he submits to the will of the superior; because it is by him that God speaks.

It is therefore true that the religious life possesses an inexhaustible store of merits; and this is what our Saviour meant when he said to a young man: If you wish to be perfect, follow me, and you will have treasures in Heaven. The reward of him who keeps the commandments in the world is Heaven; but the reward of him who follows the counsels in a religious life, is treasure in Heaven.

Some one asked St. Eugidius, if seculars could acquire perfection. He replied: ". They can, but I prefer one degree of grace in religion, where it is easy to increase, and difficult to lose it, to ten degrees in the world, where it is difficult to increase, and easy to lose it." St. Lawrence Justinian said, that if God would clearly show seculars the advantages of a religious life, all would fly to it with a haste which would depopulate the world.   Happy ye who are called to so great a felicity!   Give God eternal praise and thanks.   *Bless ye the Lord, O! all his chosen ones, keep days of joy and give him praise.*   If you feel inclined to the religious state, my dear reader, before fixing your choice, examine the difficulties which I shall place before you in the following chapter, so as not to imitate him who buys land without reflecting whether it will conduce to his pleasure, or without thinking of the money and labor he must expend thereon.

CHAPTER XVI.

SECTION 1. *Which of the three states is the most
perfect.*

MAGINE that God says to you, as he said to King David: "I give thee the choice of three things: choose one which thou wilt." It is certain that the religious state, where a person observes the Evangelical Counsels, is the most perfect state, the surest road to heaven, and the means of giving the greatest glory to God. In the other states, he cannot reach so sublime a degree of perfection, except by difficult routes. To prove to you that I do not wish to engage you in a religious life, having already cited what St. Bernard says of its advantages, I will now tell you what he says of its rigors and difficulties.

St. Bernard says, that a religious life is *a daily martyrdom*, less hard than that suffered from the executioner, but more painful by the duration of its mortifications. From the first day a person enters a monastery, he is not master of himself nor of his will, even in the

smallest things. He must submit to persons
whose characters are opposed to his own, labor
when fatigued, be still against his inclination,
interrupt the sweets of sleep. He must often
engage in menial occupations, and receive contempt for a reward. On every side there is one
cross or another awaiting a religious. Poverty
with its consequences is a continual martyrdom.
He must forsake riches with which he lived at
ease, wear a coarse habit instead of costly garments, renounce his liberty to confine himself to
a cell; leave a sumptuous table for simple and
insipid dishes that barely suffice to appease
hunger. Another combat, more violent still, is
to observe chastity. Whoever knows how violent the passions of youth are, will say with
St. Jerome: " *Chastity also has its martyrdom.*"
To preserve it, a person must always keep a
guard on his eyes, mortify his appetite, and
check his passions. Obedience, not content
with tormenting the inferior man, goes so far
as almost to martyr the heart, the soul, and the
will. It commands man to act according to the
will of others, and live as they please. There
is no one to whom he less belongs than to himself. In fine, it requires him to exercise all
virtues, to fly whatever the senses desire, to
seek whatever displeases them; generally, to
have nothing according to his liking, to be de-

prived of all that nature desires, and in a word, to bear continually the cross of Jesus Christ. See what you may expect in such a state. It is true, that good religious submit with joy on account of the love they have for God, and the hope of reward; but it is no less certain, that such a life offers many difficulties. I have not yet mentioned all. The wise man tells us, that when we enlist in the service of God we must prepare the soul for temptation. God will perhaps permit you to experience severe temptations, and to conquer them, you will be obliged to use severe penances. He will perhaps permit you to fall into so great a desolation, that you will be a burden to yourself, and will seem abandoned by God and man. It appears that the Prophet intended to refer to a religious life when he said (Ps. lxv.): "Thou, O God, hast proved us: thou hast tried us by fire, as silver is tried. Thou hast brought us into a net, thou hast laid afflictions on our back; Thou hast set men over our heads. We have passed through fire and water."

What do you think of it? Do you think I have concealed some difficulty which is to be met with in a religious life? Do not, however, throw down your arms, if God calls you to this sort of warfare; for *the Father of mercies, the God of all consolation*, does not fail, in the midst of these trials to impart strength, consolation, and contentment to Religious which cause them to love these sufferings more than the luxuries they enjoyed in the world. St. Francis of Assisium often said to his Religious: "We have promised great things to God, but God has promised greater things to us." Rely, therefore, on the tender care of his providence. Godfrey, in the flower of his age, and amid the most flattering hopes, left the world to repair with some of his friends to the monastery at Clairvaux. Being one day afflicted with an overwhelming sadness, he called to mind the relatives, friends, and riches he had abandoned. The temptation appeared exteriorly, and was perceived by one of his friends, who said to him with sweetness: "What's the matter, Godfrey?" He sighed and replied: "Alas! brother, I will never more be happy in this life." His friend mentioned this to St. Bernard, who begged God to console the afflicted. Godfrey, very much dejected, went to sleep, and awoke with a countenance so cheerful that his friend reproved him for what he had said a moment before. Godfrey replied to him: "I told you that I would never more be happy; but I sincerely hope I will never be sad again." He was really at peace after this struggle, and tasted delights in his austerities which worldlings never find in the most brilliant conditions.

Worldlings deceive themselves when they believe that the religious life is sad ; for although it may have the appearance of sadness, it really procures the most solid joy. The crosses of religious, which worldlings believe to be so intolerable, are sweet and agreeable to those who bear them. St. Paul says, that the religious, apparently most afflicted, is in reality the most consoled. "Seemingly sad but always rejoicing." Observe that before the word *sad*, he places *seemingly* ; and before the word *rejoicing*, *always*. His joy is not apparent, but solid, and often a foretaste of heavenly happiness. If sometimes he experiences extraordinary hardships in religion, the Lord proportions his grace and consolation thereto. "According to the multitude of my sorrows in my heart, thy comforts have given joy to my soul." (Ps. xciii.) God does not cause his consolations merely to equal the afflictions, but to surpass them, and St. Paul said : "I am filled with comfort, I exceedingly abound with joy in all our tribulation." (2 Cor. vii. 4.)

Charles of Lorraine, of an imperial family, in possession of a rich see, and on the point of becoming cardinal, preferred the humility of a religious life to all these dignities ; and declared, that he would willingly have made the journey to India on foot to obtain it. He there tasted delights so pure, that the shortest of these agreeable moments repaid him a hundred-fold for all he left in the world. Urban VIII. asked him, how he succeeded in his new state. "Most holy father," replied he, "I blush to confess it: I am transported by so great a joy, that I cannot refrain from expressing it by singing canticles in my cell: How lovely are thy tabernacles, O God of virtues! my soul panteth and fainteth after the courts of the Lord; my heart and my body leap with joy in thinking of the living God."

SECTION 2. *Greater advantages of the most perfect state.*

A RELIGIOUS life, says St. Augustine, is not a sad life, as worldlings think; but according to the words of Jesus Christ, it procures for those who have left all for it, a hundred-fold in this world, and eternal happiness in the next. Peace of heart and the tranquillity of a good conscience, are worth a hundred times all the consolations of the world. Seculars themselves often say, when they visit a monastery: How happy these religious are! they enjoy in their cloister a profound calm, which is the image of that in heaven, and which forms a striking contrast with the tempests that continually agitate us in the world. "O happy they, if they but knew their bliss!"

The hope alone of eternal rewards, when there is no temporal advantage, gives the poor of Jesus Christ far more contentment, than the possession of all perishable goods can procure for the rich. The dignity, the honor, the sovereignty, bestowed upon the poor in spirit, is worth more than all the treasures of the world. As it is a disgrace to the rich to become the slaves of worldly wealth, so also is it a great honor for these poor in spirit, to be exempted from such a tyranny, and acquire, in abandoning these goods, that dominion which others strive in vain to gain whilst possessing them. Arnulf of Citeaux, who left the immense riches and honors of a court to retire into a poor monastery, often exclaimed: "What thou hast said, sweet Jesus, is true; thou wilt accomplish thy promises." He was asked, what he meant by this exclamation. "I speak," said he, "of the hundred-fold promised to those who have abandoned all for the love of God, and I experience its unquestionable effects, in abandoning all I possess."

Do you fear that you will shorten your days by the rigors of penance? St. Romuald lived a hundred years amidst the greatest austerities; and in his countenance was always seen the expression of that joy which replenished his heart. Urban V. thought to mitigate the penances of the Cistercians; John of Villanova presented to him eighty of them who, after their profession, had lived eighty years in good health. If it is hard to leave the delights of the world, and embrace the cross of Jesus, it is, however, true of all religious, as St. Bernard says of his, that they taste so many consolations in their mortifications, as to make them fear lest God, having rewarded them in this life by a sort of Paradise, may deprive them of its enjoyments in the life to come. But this fear is void of foundation, for one of the greatest consolations of religion is the certain hope it gives of eternal salvation. St. Chrysostom says: "God cannot deceive: he has promised eternal life to those who leave all; you have abandoned all, therefore he will give you eternal life. How can you fear the result of his promises?" St. Bernard speaks as clearly: "From the cell to heaven, the way is easy; it will seldom happen that a religious will pass from the cell to hell; for, he alone will end his life in a cell, who is destined to enter heaven." "One begins to enter heaven," says St. Lawrence Justinian, "when he consecrates himself to a religious life; for this is a manifest sign of predestination. Some saints to whom God has revealed that they would be saved, have been inebriated with joy: why would it not be so with religious to whom Jesus Christ himself has promised eternal glory?"

The assurance of salvation is also founded on this: the religious life is the preservation from future sins and the baptism for sins committed. St. Jerome, St. Anselm, and St. Bernard, assure us, that when one enters religion, he receives the same graces as when baptized. St. Anselm, in an ecstasy, saw himself led to the gates of heaven; the devils tried to prevent his entering, by accusing him of sins committed in the world, but the angel replied: "Accuse him, if you can, of faults committed in religion! for when he made his vows, all he had committed in the world were pardoned." It is a great consolation to a soul defiled by sin, to know that entrance into religion will be a second baptism, with the aid of which she will cancel all her debts to God, great as they may be.

The holy doctors have therefore had great reasons for bestowing eulogies upon the religious state, and for calling it the life of angels, the theatre of virtues, the paradise of joys, the pledge of eternal happiness. It is then with great wisdom that millions of persons,—princes, great men of the world, kings, heirs of thrones,

14

— to gain all by the rich nothing of religious poverty, have cast aside the royal mantles, placed their crowns and sceptres at the foot of the crucifix, and have found their glory and delight in the ignominy and bitterness of the cross.

PART SECOND.

OF A WISE CHOICE IN PARTICULAR.

 HAVE thus far treated of a wise choice in general; I will now treat of the means of conquering the difficulties which generally oppose such a choice. It would be too tedious to write in detail on every state, and I will therefore confine myself especially to the religious state; not that I wish to draw to it the person who is choosing, but because this state being the most difficult to embrace, its difficulties being removed, the obstacles to embracing any other state will, for a still greater reason, be also removed. Solve the more difficult, and the more easy solve themselves. It is for you to apply to other states, what I may say of the religious life.

CHAPTER I.

SECTION 1. *Of the different kinds of religious life.*

HERE are persons whom the Holy Ghost calls to an Order, especially designed for them; as St. Nicholas Tolentino was called to the Institute of St. Augustine, St. Hyacinth to that of St. Dominic, St. Bonaventure to that of St. Francis, and St. Stanislaus to the Society of Jesus. However, it often happens, that a person, having resolved to embrace the religious state, does not know what Order to join, nor whether to consecrate himself to a solitary and contemplative life, or to one that is mixed. When the Devil sees that any one aspires to perfection, he endeavors to seduce him, either by leading him into situations where perfection is not found, or by exciting him to undertake a burden so heavy that he will be unable to bear it. To avoid these snares, two things must be considered: first, the temperament or disposition

160

of the person choosing; secondly, the constitution of the religious Order he desires to embrace. In fact, grace adapts itself to nature: those in whom a melancholy disposition prevails, who love repose and retirement, feel drawn to solitude and to the desert. As soon as St. Jerome had left the abodes of men, and found himself alone, he cried out: "Let no one speak to me again of the dissipation of cities, or of the troubles of the world. I am here delivered from a thousand snares, from many occasions of sin. I converse alone, and when I wish with God. Relatives and friends no longer entertain me with their prosperity, nor speak to me of their adversity. No more of reverses of fortune, or changes of state, or threats of war, or visits of ceremony. I have to think only of God and myself. I find here my delight and a foretaste of Paradise. Oh! happy solitude! Oh! singular blessedness!"

Others of a sterner nature, though not so fond of solitude, are very desirous of mortifying themselves by bodily penances, and are called to the Order of Capuchins, or the barefooted Carmelites. St. Bonaventure, knowing that wisdom does not exist amongst those who live at their ease, found his consolation in conquering his body by austerities. Some seem born to shed blessings around them, and desire the mixed life, such as

14*

is found in the Order of St. Dominic, or in that
of St. Francis, or in others newly instituted.
Such was the inclination of St. Augustine.   He
compared to the Angels, those who contemplate
God, and at the same time labor for the salvation of their neighbor.

You will perhaps ask me which of these Orders
is the most perfect?   St. Thomas says, it is that
which most resembles the life of Jesus Christ
and his Apostles, who joined contemplation with
the care of souls.   " Those religious orders possess the highest degree of perfection which are
instituted both to teach and preach; for it is
more meritorious to impart light to others, than
merely to glitter."   So that the Order he most
esteemed, was that which joined to the observance of the evangelical counsels, labors of great
merit: such as preaching, administering the
sacraments, instructing the ignorant, reclaiming
wanderers, converting heretics and infidels at
the cost of the severest labors.   St. Thomas
says, moreover, that it is a work of great perfection to teach the sciences — as the Dominicans
and Franciscans do — in order to promote faith
and piety amongst seculars, by forming to virtue
the young persons whose studies they direct.
The saint even adds, that the occupation of
teaching and leading others to virtue is more
estimable than martyrdom, *secundum propriam*

speciem actûs. Jesus Christ has revealed, that those who, by writing or by teaching, labor for the salvation of souls and the glory of God, do good which may last through all ages, and the whole of which will contribute to their own sal- . vation. Those who teach others the road to salvation, shall shine as stars for all eternity (Daniel xii. 3). St. Chrysostom gives as a reason for it, that we procure God more pleasure and glory by gaining a single soul, than by abandoning an entire world of wealth. It is on this account that monks, especially the Benedictines, give their lives to the education of youth, and to a thousand other means of helping their neighbor.

SECTION 2. *One ought to choose the Order most suited to his own dispositions.*

THE most perfect states do not suit all men. The arms of Saul only embarrassed the young David. St. Ambrose says: "Let every one study his natural disposition and learn what good and what evil it contains, and also his inclination for practising virtue and avoiding vice; for a person generally acquits himself best of those employments for which he has a natural disposition, and is more contented with them. The occupation pleases him, and the pleasure he takes in it helps him to succeed." Examine then your dispositions of mind and body. Perhaps your strength would fail you in one Order, whilst it would suffice for another. Perfection does not consist in austerity—which is only a means and not an end—but in a denial of self-will. "It is far more meritorious," says St. Gregory, "to submit *our will to another's than to chastise the body with severe austerities.*" If you are inclined to bodily penances, you can practise them every where with discretion. In Orders regarded as less austere, there are many Religious who practise the most rigid austerities. To make a wise choice of a religious Order you must avoid two stumbling-blocks: the first is that of entering an Order because you have a relative or a friend there who promises to protect, promote, and help you. These motives are unworthy of a courageous youth who wishes to leave the world. If you seek riches and ease, enjoy them at home. The second stumbling-block is that of entering a degenerate Order, to live there in liberty. Rather preserve your liberty in the world, than bind yourself by vows, the violation of which would be a sacrilege. If you ask me which are the degenerate Orders, I will in reply only remind you of the words of the great Constantine: "If I should see a Priest commit a fault, I would endeavor to cover it with my imperial mantle." You would inform yourself on this subject, by conversing with different Religious, by examining their discourse, and their conduct, and by seeing whether they have fraternal charity, are obedient, and possessed of delicate consciences. See whether they are ambitious or humble, circumspect or careless in their intercourse with the world, and whether they speak of spiritual or worldly things. Their language will let you know them.

Finally, it would be wrong for you to avoid an Order which has produced many great men, through fear of not being esteemed in it. This would be an ambition unworthy of a step which ought to be founded on humility. St. Anselm was sometimes tormented with this temptation; but one day at prayer, God suggested this thought to him: "What! when one has become a Religious, ought he desire to be superior to others and seek honors? I ought, on the contrary, to choose precisely the place in which I will be most humbled, and regarded as the last of all." He immediately repaired to a monastery. But to reward his humility, God gave him learning, and he shone amongst Doctors as a sun amid stars.

CHAPTER II.

SECTION 1. *Rules for ascertaining whether a vocation comes from God, or not.*

OUNG people are sometimes at a loss to know, whether it is God or the devil that urges them to a particular state. I will give you three rules by which you may recognize the voice of God:

First, when God excites the soul by such an abundance of graces, that there no longer remains any doubt as to whether it is his voice or not. It happened thus with St. Matthew and St. Paul.

The second is, when the impression is not so strong, nor the certainty so positive, but still the interior movement of the heart is so powerful that you can have almost a perfect certainty.

And, thirdly, when, the mind being clear of every bias, and exempt from the troubles that might deceive or disturb the judgment, you decide tranquilly by the light of eternal truths,

upon a state which you clearly see to be the best
for you.

But to obtain a more perfect certainty, you
must reflect chiefly on your motives for embracing the state you are considering. In fact,
the religious state is not the last end, but a
means which may serve different ends. If, then,
your motive for entering the religious state is
to promote your spiritual welfare therein; for
example, to be delivered from the dangers of the
world, to reform your conduct, to observe the
evangelical counsels, to enjoy the peace of a
good conscience, or to insure your salvation;
then it is certain that the vocation comes from
God. The reason is, that no carnal affection is
mingled with these motives; all is founded on
the love of spiritual things. This love cannot
come from nature, nor from the devil; it must
therefore come from God. It cannot be the
effect of our corrupt nature, for this nature in-
cites us to the gratification of our senses, to the
desire of riches and pleasure, and flies from all
mortification and submission to the orders of
another. It cannot come from the devil, because
he never acts against himself; he never seeks to
destroy the sway which he wishes to exercise
over souls. If the devil could possibly inspire
us to quit the world, and give ourselves to God;
to renounce sensual pleasures, and embrace the

rigors of penance, he would be against himself;
he would be destroying his empire which consists in insinuating into our hearts a love for
pleasures and honors. Therefore, it is not
credible that the devil can be the author of these
holy thoughts.

But perhaps you will say, that the devil often
transforms himself into an angel of light, the
better to deceive us; that he wishes to lead us
into religion in order afterwards to make us
leave it, with a disgust for holy things; that
many, having entered religion, have lived scan-
dalously in it, and have left it with disgrace;
and you will, finally, conclude not to embrace
the religious state. No conclusion more errone-
ous than this. Bankers pursue their business,
although many have been made bankrupt by it;
soldiers enter the army, although many have
lost their lives in it, some have deserted, and
others have left it in disgrace; young persons
study, although some have lost their health
by doing so; the nobility frequent the court,
although many have there met with disappointment. The same may be said of all other states.
Why then should we not embrace the Religious
state, although some persons conduct themselves
improperly in it, or leave it? Soldiers without
the least hesitation expose their lives for a few
dollars per month; bankers risk their fortune,

and students their health. Shall we, then, expose our lives for a temporal advantage, and risk nothing — if indeed there is any risk — in the surest road to heaven and eternal happiness? Why not rather consider the far greater number of persons who persevere in religion, and live there holily? Why should not their perseverance inspire more confidence than the fall of others causes fear?

Some persons judge by the issue, whether vocations are true or false. When a person remains in the religious state until death, they regard it as certain that he has been called to it by the Holy Ghost. If another casts down his arms, they declare that he was not called by divine inspiration. "Beautiful reasoning, this!" says St. Thomas, "the failure to persevere does not prove that one has not been called by God; for then it would be necessary to maintain that all divine favors are permanent and perpetual, and that when a person has once received grace, he can never lose it; now this would be to maintain a downright heresy."

If it could be said, that the devil invites souls to a religious life in order to destroy them, it might also be said, that he calls Pagans to the faith in order to plunge them afterwards into heresy. But who would believe that conversion to the faith comes from the devil? The Holy

15

Scriptures, the Councils, and history teach us, that many have at first obeyed the vocation of God, and have afterwards ended badly through their own fault. Our Saviour, whilst preaching in .Judea, invited all men, saying: Come and follow me; yet, how many of those that obeyed so evident a vocation did not persevere; for *" many of his disciples went back, and walked no more with him."* And whom do we find among them? Judas — an apostle — afterwards an apostate and traitor! Would you, on this account, have declined following Christ if you had lived in those times? The devil is not so false to his own cause as to bring a soul into religion, where he is sure of losing it, or, at least, of winning it with great difficulty, whilst it is so easy for him to conquer in the world, where it is exposed without protection. He very cunningly makes use of the inconstancy of a few to supply others with false reasons for declining to enter the religious state.

SECTION 2. *Human motives of a vocation.*

I HAVE shown, according to St. Thomas, that the inspiration which is accompanied with virtuous motives can come only from God. But Lessius goes farther, and says, that even when one of the motives for entering religion is a temporal object,—for instance, to flee worldly occupa-

tions and enjoy a pious repose, to escape from
domestic calamities, to avoid the reproach which
for some cause we meet with when we appear
in public, and other motives of a similar nature,
it must be held that such a vocation comes from
the Holy Ghost; for the influence of some human
motive does not destroy the merit of a work
done for God, as may be seen by the earthly
rewards He so often promised and gave in the
Old Testament. . We see proofs of it in many
persons. St. Arsenius became a religious to
escape the snares which his disciple, the Emperor Arcadius, laid for him. The two Pauls, the
glory of the desert, retired thither, the one to
avoid the persecution of a relative who coveted
his inheritance, the other to avoid the shame
of living with a faithless wife. St. Romuald,
founder of the Camaldolenses, repaired to the
cloister, because, having been witness to a
murder committed in a duel by Sergius, his
father, he wished to escape the rigor of the law.
He withdrew to the monastery as a place of
safety, was touched by the sweet conversation
and happy life of the religious, and gave himself entirely to God. These persons made a
virtue of necessity, became great saints, and
could say with St. Augustine, "Happy fault,
which has brought us to better things." St.
Thomas adds, that even when we suppose the

thought of quitting the world to be inspired by the devil, it would be well to follow the counsel ; as no one would refuse a large sum of money, because it is paid by an enemy, nor a beautiful picture, because it is executed by an immoral painter ; for we do not then regard the giver, but the gift. If the devil were the author of the vocation, you could, like David, boast of having killed Goliath with his own sword.

We may have a sufficient certainty that the vocation comes from God. It is not necessary that an angel should come down from heaven to intimate to you the will of God. You ought not to desire such revelations, especially when there is question of consecrating yourself to God. There is not so much danger in closely following Jesus Christ that you must needs have positive orders, direct from heaven, to avoid being deceived. It is, on the contrary, very true, that if you ought to ask God for revelations on either side of the question, you should rather ask, whether you can safely remain in the world, than whether you can safely leave it. Indeed, Jesus Christ exhorts us to embrace poverty ; he has wished to give us a dread of riches and of the world. Therefore St. Thomas says, one must have special reasons for staying in the world. How then can those be deceived who wish to leave it? When a person is to begin a voyage, he does not deliberate as to whether he shall trust his life to a vessel that is unseaworthy, or to one that is entirely safe — why, therefore, when he embarks for eternity, are so many reasons necessary to lead him into the surest state of life?

They who desire particular motives may consider those I have advanced, especially when the vocation rests on spiritual and eternal motives. As for the rest, the ways of Divine Providence are admirable: at one time he calls us by the voice of a preacher who touches our hearts; at another time by pious reading, or by the advice of a confessor, or by the interior emotions we experience after Holy Communion.

A person's vocation may arise from his being scoffed at by his companions, which fills him with disgust for the world; that of another from having a difficulty or from meeting with an injury, escaping a danger, or being afflicted with a disease. God, says St. Augustine, acts like a nurse who rubs her breasts with wormwood when she wishes to wean her infant, in order that the child may find only bitterness where it expected only sweetness. It often happens, says St. Macarius, that God sends tribulations and reverses, that you may conclude from them; "Since the deceitful world does not give me what I wish, I abandon it; I cast myself upon

15*

the bosom of God, who will never deceive me."

SECTION 3. *Examples of extraordinary vocations.*

ST. ANTHONY, assisting at Mass, heard these words read from the Gospel : "*If thou wilt be perfect, go sell what thou hast, and give to the poor,*" (Matt. xix. 21) ; he immediately took the advice to himself, and followed it.

St. Francis Borgia, after the death of the Empress, saw her face, which, though in life so beautiful, had become so hideous that he could scarce recognize it. This sight made him sensible of the nothingness of human things ; and he resolved, no longer to serve a master subject to death, but to give himself at once to God.

Thomas Pond—an English nobleman—possessed of all the qualities that render a youth amiable, repaired at the age of twenty to the court of Queen Elizabeth, of England, who loaded him with favors. One day, at a ball, he danced with such ease and elegance as to charm all the noble assembly ; and the queen herself, as a sign of her satisfaction, took him by the hand and bade him rest a while. Elizabeth invited Pond again to show his talent at another ball, but, whilst dancing, he was seized with a dizziness and fell. The spectators burst into laughter,

and the queen, indignant at seeing the feat fail,
said contemptuously in Latin, " *Surge, Domine
Bos.*" " Get up, my lord Bull." He answered:
" *Sic transit gloria mundi.*" " *Thus passes the
glory of the world.* See how it repays the
trouble one takes for it." He left the court,
retired to his palace, devoted himself to prayer,
penance, and good works, and finally embraced
the religious state. He practised great virtues
there, and showed such a constancy in the faith
that he very willingly suffered for it in ten different prisons.

The eldest son of a baron of the empire, affected by the death of one of his young friends,
retired to Clairvaux, without saying anything
to his parents about it. His father — a very
distinguished officer — who designed that this
son should take a high post in the army, as
soon as he heard this news, ran in fury to the
monastery, and threatened to destroy the house
and community. The youth was obliged to
appear before his father, but excused his conduct by saying, that he had fled because he
could not endure a bad custum that prevailed
in his country; but that if his father, by his
authority as marquis, would abolish this terrible custom, he would very willingly return to
enjoy the delights of his paternal roof. The
father replied, that his son had only to speak,

and whatever displeased him should be instantly suppressed. "This custom," replied the youth, "which offends me is, that young people die as well as old men; if you remedy this, I will return with you." The father, surprised, saw that his power did not extend so far: at the same time God touched his heart; he dismissed his servants and remained himself at Clairvaux.

Peter Gonzales, the nephew of the Archbishop of Palenzo, was much addicted to the fashionable follies of youth. On a certain day when he was to enter into a high office, he appeared in public with an extraordinary pageant. As he was riding through the principal street, his horse fell and threw him in the mud. His companions and the passers-by could not suppress their laughter at the ridiculous figure he made, whilst he, confused and humbled, hastily concealed himself from the public gaze. This accident affected him so deeply, that he was never seen in public afterwards. By the grace of God, he was enabled to see the vanities of the world in their proper light. Disgusted with them, he entered the order of St. Dominic, and became a saint. Like St. Paul, he was first prostrated to the earth, that he might afterwards be raised to heaven. "God is wonderful in his saints;" his wisdom supplies him with an infinite variety of means for procuring the salvation of men.

CHAPTER III.

SECTION 1. *Bad habits do not free us from embracing a perfect state of life.*

E see men so faint-hearted, or rather so disposed to give way to temptations, that, after examining the great advantages of the religious state, instead of feeling incited to embrace it, they flee from it through a false humility. It seems to them, that they could never conquer the bad habits formed in the world, and they remain in it through a fear of having to return to it, in case they should enter religion. To these I say: if you wish to save your soul, you surely know that you must conquer these bad habits. Pray tell me then, where do you hope to succeed more easily? Is it in the world, where these very habits were contracted, and where you have seen by experience that licentious manners and dangerous occasions have so often caused you to offend God, and perhaps so grievously that you no longer feel any remorse? Or is it

in the religious state, where, by acts of virtue, and the help of good example, you can remove all bad habits and acquire those that are good? How numerous are the means religion affords for subduing your passions, whilst the world does not furnish one!

St. Thomas inquires, whether persons not yet exercised in the practice of the precepts, should enter religion. After adducing the remedies which religion offers for impurity, ambition, and intemperance, he concludes with reason, that immediately after the conversion of a vicious person, he can enter the cloister, even though he still have bad habits which follow and cling to him, and which, as St. Augustine says of his own vices, cry after him: "Ah! leave us not, forsake not your old friends; you will not be able to live without us." Despise their clamors; you will find in the monastery a good school for learning to fight and subdue them. Do not doubt, therefore, that you are called by God; on the contrary, be assured that divine goodness wishes to rid your soul, in the cloister, of its vices, which perhaps would always increase if you should be exposed to the dangers of the world. But if you fear that you are risking too much, consult your spiritual father.

A manly heart can easily conquer bad habits in the cloister, where they lose half their vio-

lence, and where religion provides her followers with powerful weapons. As bad habits
acquire strength by frequent acts, so by leaving
off those acts, they dwindle away little by little.
Now, by the very act of leaving the world, a
person renounces these vicious habits, and, in
consequence, begins to exercise the contrary
virtues; by opposing mortification to incon-
tinency, sobriety to intemperance, and poverty to the love of riches. It will therefore be
easy to banish bad inclinations, and adopt the
contrary virtues.

The sole advantage of conversing and asso-
ciating with good people produces a love for
virtue; and love begets a desire of practising
it; and thus, you will advance in virtue without
perceiving it; just as the lion taken from the
forest and kept for some time amongst men,
gradually loses his ferocity, and insensibly
assumes almost another nature.

If the nature and industry of man can of
themselves effect much, what will they not
accomplish when reinforced by the grace of
God! If you had to reform your habits by
your own strength alone, you would surely
have reason to fear; but God with his almighty
power will assist you, and will give you grace
to renounce your vices. He knows how to
straighten what is crooked, and to smooth what

is rough. Confide in Him, for his word is
pledged to help you. Fear not, says he, for
I am with you; I have strengthened you; I
have aided you; all those who fight against
you shall be confounded, they shall be as if
they were not. O! how admirably the grace
of God reforms the will and the other powers
of the souls of those on whom it descends!
These sudden changes in the servants of God
would hardly be credible, if we did not see
them in others and experience them in ourselves. A person often thinks he could not
live, if deprived of this or that pleasure; yet,
after a little while he renounces it, and cannot
even think of it again without horror. Who
does not admire the power of the Lord, when
he sees men once cruel, intemperate, avaricious,
and ambitious, now mild, temperate, poor in
spirit, and humble of heart? Come and see
the works of the Lord and the wonders he
performs on earth. What do you fear, says
St. Bernard, you whose feeble hearts are filled
with despondency? Is it that the Lord is
unwilling to pardon your sins? but he has
nailed them to the cross with his hands. Do
you fear that you will not succeed because
you are composed of frail clay? but God who
made you, knows your weakness. Do you
fear that your bad habits have bound you

hand and foot? but Almighty God can break your chains. Do you fear that God will refuse you his grace on account of your past sins? he did not come to call the just, but sinners; whom he loves most tenderly, not because they are sinners, but because he sees what they will become with his help; just as a great sculptor cherishes in a rough piece of marble the beautiful statue his chisel will shape from it.

SECTION 2. *St. Augustine victorious over bad habits.*

FROM among a thousand examples I would cite to prove the possibility of correcting bad habits, I select that of St. Augustine, whose conversion is known by his own writings. He for a long time delayed giving himself to God, and a little boat in the tempest-lashed sea could not be more agitated than his heart was, in the continual struggle between the flesh and the spirit. He desired to withdraw himself from sensual pleasures, and sometimes had recourse to God, but without wishing to be heard. He desired continence, provided God would not give it to him too soon, and would let him have a few more days to indulge in his disorderly pleasures. Now and then, he nobly ran to embrace the Cross of Jesus Christ; but as soon as he beheld it, his resolution failed him.

16

He wished to escape from his shameful vices,
but it seemed to him impossible to live without
them.   I was bound, says he, by trifles and
vanities, those dear old associates who would
whisper to me : Do you then wish to leave us?
Can it be that from this moment we will never
more be with you?   Do you then think yourself able to live, not for years, but even one
single instant without these carnal pleasures,
to which you are so accustomed that they are
almost identified with your nature?   Augustine
sighed ; he was bound, not by an iron chain,
but by an iron will.   He did not even understand how he could be chaste and continent.

Fatigued by these long and violent agitations,
he one day said to himself: Why can you not do
what so many other men and women have done
in positions like yours?   They have not conquered by their own strength, but by the help
they have received from God.   Do as they did.
Confide in God.   Cast yourself into his arms ;
for this tender father will not withdraw his
hands and let you fall, but will press you to
his bosom, and heal you.   Finally, Augustine
boldly renounced his vices, and gave himself
without reserve to God, who expelled these false
pleasures from his heart, and took their place.
In transports of joy, he tasted all the sweetness
of this new life, understood how vain, how ruin-

ous to his soul, and how abominable were the
objects to which he was before attached, and
exclaimed with a lively gratitude: Lord, thou
hast broken my bonds, I will eternally praise
thy power and thy mercy.

Imitate this great model, and be persuaded,
that the greater your repugnance to leaving vice,
the greater will be your joy for having left it.

Consider the admirable example of so many
others, who with the aid of grace have triumphed over the pleasures of sense. Why may
you not hope for the same favors from God?

Although you have not been able to gain the
victory in the midst of the world and its dangerous occasions, be assured, that, in disengaging
yourself from these snares by a religious profession, you will succeed. It will be with you
as with St. Felicitas, who groaned in prison
under the pains of childbirth, and yet rejoiced
whilst enduring the torments of martyrdom.
Being asked the reason, she replied: when I
was giving birth to my child, nature acted in
me, but at the torture the grace of God was my
support. What nature believes impossible, grace
makes easy and sweet. Say then with confidence: *I can do all things in him who strength-
eneth me.* (Phil. iv. 13.)

CHAPTER IV.

SECTION 1. *Ought we to obey the divine call, notwithstanding the opposition of parents?*

MANY authors have shown how great a sin it is for parents to oppose the vocation of their children, to shut the way of salvation against them, and to destroy not only their offspring, but themselves also. I will here consider only those youths who, through a false respect for their parents, do not obey the call of God. To these I say: you have too tender an attachment to your parents; you wish to obey them to the prejudice of the divine mandates. In the Gospel, Jesus Christ says, *he who loves father or mother more than me, is not worthy of me.* St. Bernard declares that a person is in this situation, when through respect for his parents, he does not follow the invitation of Jesus Christ. Just imagine that you are called at the same time by Jesus Christ on the one side, and by your parents on the other: both tell you how tenderly they love you, what they deserve from

you, and the rewards prepared for you. But
how vast a difference! The love of Jesus, his
merits and 'rewards are heavenly, immense, and
eternal; those of your parents are earthly, weak,
and inconstant. The apostle says: *Children,
obey your parents in the Lord,* but not against
the Lord. They ought to be obeyed, so far as
their commands are not opposed to those of
God; for if they go beyond this, they are not
fathers, but murderers of their own offspring.

Let us see what the holy fathers think on this
point. St. Jerome in writing to young Heliodorus, who, through attachment to his family, had
left the service of God, says: What, delicate soldier, are you doing in your father's house?
Should your little nephew cling to your neck,
your tender mother present herself with di-
shevelled hair and torn garments, and show you
the breast which nourished you; should your
father, to stop you, stretch himself upon the
threshold, flee to the standard of the cross, and
fear not that, by this, you are wanting in the
duty you owe your parents; for it is an act—
not of cruelty—but of affection. The same
saint says elsewhere: Your father will be afflicted, but Jesus will be rejoiced; your family
will weep, but the angels will congratulate you.
Let your father do as he pleases with his property; your parents seek not your interest, but

16 *

their own. Indeed, their tears often flow, not from the love they bear their children, but from the grief of being deprived of the' advantages and honors they hoped to obtain through them.

St. Augustine writes to Lœtus, a wealthy young man, who, through love for his parents, was wanting in resolution: The heavenly trumpet calls you to a spiritual warfare; but you are delayed by an irregular attachment to your mother. What is the cause of this attachment? Has she pressed you to her bosom in your helpless infancy? bestowed unceasing care upon your education? Do not permit these tender thoughts to lead you astray, but leave your mother for a little while, that you may eternally enjoy her company in heaven. St. Bernard exhorts the young Walter to leave the world. He was distinguished as well by his talents, as by his birth, but was too much attached to his mother. I give you the words of the saint: What shall I reply to you? Shall I tell you to leave your mother? but this would seem inhuman. To remain with her? but it will not be to her interest to cause the loss of your soul. Shall I advise you to serve the world and Jesus Christ at the same time? but it is a declaration of eternal truth, that *no man can serve two masters.* Choose then, either to gratify your mother's will, or to procure her salvation and your own. It may be said, that although it is sinful in a person to despise his mother, yet it is meritorious to do so for the love of God; since he who said: *Honor thy father and thy mother;* says also: *He who loves father or mother more than me, is not worthy of me.*

SECTION 2. *The love of Jesus triumphs over the love of parents.*

THE sentiments of the holy doctors have been followed by many. St. Fulgentius, the only son of a distinguished lady, secretly fled to a convent. When his mother learned it, she hastened to the convent and there repeatedly called aloud for her beloved son, but no one replied to her. She seated herself at the door, and continually repeated his name, exclaiming: "Come, O! darling of my soul! return, thou only hope of my family." His constancy was shaken by the affliction of his mother, but by praying to God, he obtained His help, and triumphed over flesh and blood.

St. Thomas of Aquin, in the flower of youth, retired to a monastery of St. Dominic, without even taking leave of the countess his mother, or of his brothers. His mother went to Naples to see him, but he fearing his inability to resist the tender violence of a mother's love, asked the prior to send him immediately to Paris. When his mother heard that he was gone, she sent his brothers in pursuit of him. On his return, she tempted him in every possible manner, mingling threats with caresses, and tears with reproaches. The holy young man listened with respect, because she was his mother, but replied with a modest firmness, that he was obliged to obey God rather than her. The mother, seeing how useless were all her efforts, sent his two sisters to employ the most tender entreaties to overcome his constancy. They having failed, she delivered him to two of his brothers, who imprisoned him for two years in a tower, and there tormented him with every species of cruelty. But the tears of a mother, the cruelty of his brothers, and the tenderness of his sisters, only confirmed him in his resolution, and he finally escaped by a window and fled to the Dominican convent.

St. Aloysius, marquis of Chatillon, said, that there was nothing in this world that he loved more affectionately than he did his parents; he, however, had the courage to leave them. He begged them for three years to give their consent, and shed many tears to obtain it. The love of Jesus Christ is far more powerful than the love of parents.

Observe, however, that when parents oppose

a choice, I do not in general praise those youths who, by an indiscreet fervor, fly to a convent without asking their consent; this must be done only by an evident inspiration. But obstacles must be conquered by prayer, by entreaty, and by patience.

To him who desires the religious state, his home is a prison, and the opposition of parents only tends to strengthen his resolution; and God at last crowns his patience with the favor desired. Indeed, if your parents see, that at home you have pious habits, that you are recollected, and speak only of spiritual things, that you dispise vanities, and delight in pious reading, devotion to prayer and penance, and frequent the sacraments, that you have patience and constancy under reproaches and contradiction, they will give you the permission you desire, and will say, with the parents of St. Aloysius: Go, my child; you are born to serve, not the world, but God. This is the surest course, and by pursuing it, if your vocation is well founded, you will resist all attacks. If, after all your mild and respectful exertions, you cannot soften the hearts of your parents, ask your spiritual father if it would be well to imitate the young Elias who retired to the monastery at Clairvaux without mentioning it to his parents, and caused St. Bernard to write to them the following letter:

The only reason for not obeying one's father is God; for he says: He who loves father or mother more than me, is not worthy of me. If you love me like good parents, why disturb me, when I do all I can to obey God, my eternal Father! why do you wish to withdraw me from the service of him, to serve whom is to reign? when it is evident that one's enemies are those of his own household, he cannot obey them, even though they be parents. All I have received from you, is my being born in sin, and brought forth in affliction. If you love me, you will rejoice that I fly to my heavenly Father. Why do you wish to make me a child of Satan? Is it not cruel to desire my ruin, when I desire my salvation? to draw me into the flames of the world, when I have but barely escaped their violence? O! how strange! the house burns, and you wish to have me within its blazing walls,—to persuade me who am safe, to return to you who do not trouble yourselves with your salvation, but who wish to involve me in your ruin. What shall I then do? shall I go to console my mother, so that we may weep together without consolation for all eternity? shall I go to appease the wrath of my father, and afterwards share his eternal grief? The only wise course I can take, is to serve God, to renounce worldly pleasures for those that are heavenly. Then cease, dear parents, cease your afflictions and cease to re-call me. Your importunities remove me further from you.' The cloister will always be the place of my repose. I will dwell there, because I have chosen it. I will pray for the pardon of my sins and yours; and I hope to obtain of God, that after a short separation for the love of him, we will be eternally reunited and happy in heaven."

CHAPTER V.

SECTION 1. *To defer the execution of a choice is almost the same as to abandon it.*

ONE of the most dangerous temptations — and which is not thought to be one — is to delay the execution of a choice, for reasons which are only the promptings of self-love in disguise; for example, great undertakings must be matured, lest by being hastily done they may not succeed, — you must first see things put in order, and a thousand other matters attended to. These are so many tricks of the devil, who wishes to interpose these delays, hoping that by disobedience to your vocation, you may finally lose the way to Heaven. Therefore, when you have not a strong reason for delay, and one which is approved of by your spiritual Father, carry out your good design as soon as possible; for experience teaches, that youths rarely maintain the fervor of vocation for a long time. A witticism from a companion, or a few words from a relative are sometimes sufficient

to stifle the good thought. Good desires easily
vanish during the time of vacation; for in the
world it is easy to lose grace, and very easy
for the fervor of charity to subside; and, consequently, it is not difficult to lose therein the
impulse given by the Holy Ghost, who is
grieved by even slight faults.

St. Thomas asks, if it is allowable to defer
one's entrance into religion? He replies, and
proves, that a person should enter as soon as
possible. But we see it clearly enough in the
Gospel. When Peter and Andrew were called
by our Saviour, *immediately they left* their nets
and their father and followed Jesus. Observe
the word *immediately;* what promptness! *they
left;* what detachment!

A person in the world is continually exposed
to the danger of losing the grace of God, and
with it his vocation. Alas! what folly! cries
St. Bernard. The question is, shall I escape
the frightful depth of an infernal pit, and I take
time to reflect and ask advice before deciding.
Temptations are violent, continual, and innumerable; youth is very feeble, and already
tempted enough by corrupt nature; does not
prudence therefore exact, that we should retire
for a while into a place where there are fewer
temptations and more helps? St. Jerome said
to Paulinus: Hasten; instead of untying the

17

cord which holds your little boat in the storm,
cut it. The sea has its dangers even when
calm; but when you meet with a tempest, and
find yourself near a harbor, can you be so foolish as not to take refuge in it? A young man
in the world is like a frail boat, badly rigged,
and placed in the middle of the ocean; a
prudent choice will rescue him from this im-
minent danger. How is it, that none of his
decisions, in an affair so important and pressing,
are executed? Excessive fear of being deceived often makes us do nothing. A youth
when making a choice is perplexed; he wishes
and does not wish. To-day he says that he
will act, to-morrow he wishes a month, and
then a year, and at last does nothing. He
would wish to have — like the Angel of the
Apocalypse — one foot on land, the other on
the sea, to be at the same time in the world
and in the house of God. Such was the
situation of St. Augustine, of which he says:
I had nothing to reply, O Lord, when thou
saidst •to me: awake, thou that sleepest. I
had nothing to reply, for I was convinced of
the truth. I would utter some words like a
man half asleep. I will come presently; wait
a moment: but this *presently* never came, and
this *moment* did not end. I always resolved
to give myself to God on the morrow, and

never immediately." Finally, Augustine took a firm resolution, and at once embraced the cross of Jesus Christ.

The devil is never better pleased than when a person delays his entrance into religion; for then he is almost sure that he will never enter. Whatever is strong, weakens and dies with the lapse of time : now, the desire of a religious life is a strong movement against nature : therefore, he who delays to put it into execution will lose his good intentions. St. Chrysostom, preaching one day on the advantages of a religious life, concluded with these words : "Perhaps you experience a desire of this holy state; but what fruit will you draw from it, if, after having been all inflamed with this desire, you extinguish the heavenly spark by delays? Then, do not delay, otherwise it will be with you as with a traveller, who came to a stream near its source, but, frightened by its width, said : I will cross it lower down ; but the torrent became wider and deeper, and it was in the end impossible for him to cross at all. The Saviour refused a young man time to bury his father. This was a pious work and required but little time. Why this refusal ? continues the saint, the devil only seeks to insinuate himself into the soul. If he obtains a little delay, he will produce great carelessness. Then do not defer

the execution of your choice. A soul is highly
honored when God calls her to his service ; and,
to delay obedience to the call is to despise either
his wisdom, as if he were mistaken, and had
called unseasonably ; or his goodness, as if he
offered a favor not worth accepting. It is,
indeed, saying to him : " Lord, I will not follow
you now. I am not ready ; have patience, — I
will attend to it presently." Would you speak
thus to the Pope, if he should call you to a
bishopric ; or to a King, if he should appoint
you to a high office ? And is God less than
the Pope, or a King ? Can you reply to him
so impudently, without fearing that he will
abandon you ? Do you reflect that he is offering you an eternal crown in his heavenly court ?

SECTION 2. *Motives for hastening the execution*
of a choice.

DELAY deprives a person of invaluable merits
which he would daily acquire in the religious
state, and exposes him to the danger of dying
before embracing it. The greatest obstacle to a
good life, says Seneca, is to appoint the next
day for beginning it. You lose the present
which is in your power, for the future which
you cannot command. St. Bernard wrote to
Roman, who deferred giving himself to God:
Why do you put off the accomplishment of

your salutary design? Nothing is more certain than death, nothing 'more uncertain than the hour of its coming. Hasten to quit the world, and come to die the death of the just. Do not stop among sinners. How can you live where you would not wish to die? The same saint wrote to a youth, named Thomas, who delayed entering the monastery: Alas! I fear lest you may imitate a young man, your namesake, who, after having resolved to enter our monastery, began to delay, and grew cold and negligent about his vocation, and was overtaken by the most sudden and frightful death.

St. Paul says: "Whosoever are led by the spirit of God they are the sons of God;" and St. Augustine says of this passage, that it belongs to the children of God, to be urged to good by a certain impetuosity of the Divine Spirit, which cannot be said of those who delay. The promptness with which a gift is offered, pleases God more than the gift itself. This Abraham and Jephtha experienced when they went to sacrifice their children. Each of these fathers tenderly loved his child, and both acted from the same motive — of pleasing God. Still, God was content with the good will of Abraham, but not with that of Jephtha. Why so? Abraham did not delay for an instant, but set out at once, and walked three days and nights

17*

to reach the mountain appointed for the sacrifice.
Jephtha, on the contrary, delayed two months,
through a love for his daughter. Abraham's
promptness pleased God, but Jephtha's delay
offended him. It is not enough to do good;
it must be done promptly. Still, we find
youths, who are anxious to consecrate themselves to God, but who wish to delay, as if
they were the dispensers of divine favors, and
could have their vocation at pleasure.

God gives inspirations in the same manner that
our Saviour bestowed his favors: *he went about
doing good.*

He does good while going about, and we
must receive it then or not at all. *Seek the
Lord,* says Isaiah, *whilst he can be found.*
If you neglect it then, you cannot succeed
when you wish. St. Augustine, in speaking
of the wedding-feast and of the workmen called
to the vineyard, says, that the master invites
people of every state, and country, and at
different hours. But, among so many different
vocations, he calls no one twice. When they
refuse, he does not send other servants to them.
We do not find that any one of the Apostles
was called more than once to follow Jesus
Christ constantly. If they had not obeyed
instantly, they would always have remained
in their miserable state. If it were as we

imagine, that what is not done to-day could be done to-morrow, Jesus Christ would not urge us so strongly to profit by the present occasion. Inspirations of God, says St. Bonaventure, are embassies which He sends us. And are there many Princes, who, when their ambassadors are refused with contempt, would send them a second time? Would they not rather dispatch armies, to avenge such an insult? God does as much; he punishes those who reject his invitations and refuse to bear his ambassadors.

CHAPTER VI.

SECTION 1. *If for strong reasons, one cannot obey his vocation immediately, he ought to be very careful to avoid all danger of losing it.*

SOMETIMES a person meets obstacles so great that he is obliged to delay the execution of his good resolutions. St. Bernard occupied the time which preceded his entrance into religion, by preparing many of his companions for entering with him. He was very amiable, and spoke so as to touch their hearts, and, consequently, he soon made many conquests. The rumor spread, and the alarm was so great, that mothers hid their children, wives their husbands, and friends their friends, for fear they would be irresistibly torn from them by the torrent of heavenly grace. But notwithstanding their precautions, as. a word from a young man has more weight than hundreds of reasons from an older person, he soon repaired to

200

Citeaux with thirty followers, as distinguished by their virtue, as by their talents, birth, and riches. I advise you in the words of the Royal Prophet, to *flee from evil and do good*.

Flee from evil, and first of all—from mortal sin; for it deprives us of grace, deserves eternal punishment, and very soon destroys the light and affections with which the Holy Ghost had designed to favor the soul. Good dispositions and holy desires are fruits that spring from sanctifying grace, as trees from the root, or as rivers from their source. If you cut the root or dry up the source, how can you expect fruits of grace, or streams of heavenly blessings? Now, to avoid mortal sin, and not to lose your vocation, you must keep far away from the paths that lead to this precipice. One of the best precautions is, to avoid the company of dissolute persons whose bad example, licentious discourse, and diabolical lessons will make you lose the grace of God. And remember, that sometimes these masked devils do not openly advise a virtuous youth to engage in evil; but they conceal the poison of their tongues, lead him gradually into their snares, and propose occasions where inexperience sees no evil, but finds hidden dangers which bring it to ruin.

These companions, says St. Ambrose, are like rocks hidden under water; we are on them and shipwrecked before we perceive them. They poison us with their very caresses. We must avoid them as we would the devil. There is no safety but in flying from them as from a plague. If our friend was infected with the plague, we would not take our recreation in his company— and still you are not afraid to spend whole days with him? Do not say, that from your experience you find these indelicate conversations, and dangerous places to be harmless. If you have not been hurt to-day, you will be to-morrow. Would you freely converse with one infected with leprosy? Suppose you are proof now against disease, will you always be so? By degrees you will be corrupted, and entirely changed; and will finally regard neither vocation, nor remorse, nor God. Your actual virtue, says St. Bernard, will no more insure you against evil, than health will against a snake with which you are trifling. Then, whoever wishes to serve God must absolutely flee from the wicked.

The second means of preserving yourself is to avoid the reading of bad books, that soil the imagination and corrupt the heart. The poison quickly enters by the eyes. But, you say, I read these authors, solely to learn to converse well, not to act badly. But soon you will be ruined without perceiving it. If you seek only beauties of style, you will find them in many excellent works. Why will you seek in the midst of dangers what you can find elsewhere with perfect safety? Then, flee from them, as from a plague. Once decided to consecrate yourself to God, you ought to avoid even the risk of a fall.

The third means is, to guard your eyes with the greatest care. Imprudent youths easily look at certain objects, without wishing to do so: the heart follows the eye, a bad impression is left on the mind, which is thus subjected to a terrible warfare. The Royal Prophet is a sad example of a dangerous look. It is for this reason that some young persons, gifted with angelic purity, such as St. Thomas and St. Aloysius, did not venture to look even their own mothers in the face.

But the beaten track to mortal sin is venial sin committed frequently and willingly. Venial sin leads to mortal sin in three ways, says St. Thomas: First, as disease disposes to death; thus, from an unguarded recreation one passes to an impure delight. Secondly, as a consequence, a person passes from one to another, so that he who does not avoid venial sin will soon commit mortal sin. He who is unfaithful in little things will soon be so in great things. Thirdly, by destroying the obstacles which prevent mortal sin. Thus, venial sin weakens virtuous habits, and renders a person unworthy of special graces. A delicate conscience and a holy fear of God are gradually destroyed by too much readiness in sinning venially.

But you will say that venial sin is light. I answer, that it is light only when compared with mortal sin. You ought not on that account fear it the less. It is always very serious of itself, since it offends a God infinitely good, and so grievously, that if you had the choice of committing a venial sin, or of suffering a very severe death, you ought to say with St. Edmund of Canterbury: I would rather be burned alive, than commit one of these faults which are called light.

God has often chastised venial sin by frightful punishments. Moses, cherished by God, was for a venial sin deprived of the happiness of entering the promised land. In like manner venial sin often hinders a person from entering the religious state. A small fault, says St. Chrysostom, brings on a great one: one laughs to excess, and sees no evil in it; to laughter succeeds jesting; to jesting, scurrility; to scurrility, free words; and then come bad actions.

A mighty conflagration arises from a little spark. A simple complaisance sometimes urges an innocent heart to commit a serious fault.

The acts are repeated and at length the virtue of purity is lost. Thus, small faults lead us on to great ones; first, because we are perverted little by little, and without at first perceiving the enormity of the evil we are approaching: secondly, because, although venial sin does not destroy charity, nor the friendship of God, still it cools it so far that often only a slight temptation will destroy it; and then it generally happens, that by losing the grace of God, we also lose our vocation.

SECTION 2. *Virtuous practices useful for preserving the desire of obeying a vocation.*

WE have explained how to shun evil: let us now see how to do good. He who aspires to the religious state ought, besides avoiding evil, to practise virtue. Above all, approach the Sacraments of Penance and the Eucharist every week, if practicable; for in these you will find all the strength necessary for fighting valiantly. Frequent communion keeps alive, and greatly increases the desire of consecrating one's self to God.

It is very essential to set aside some time in the morning of each day for meditation and prayer; and often, even in the midst of your amusements, you should repeat this prayer with your heart and your lips: " Confirm, O Lord,

18

what thou hast wrought within me." **Prayer**
is a heavenly dew, which refreshes the soul, and
strengthens its good resolution; when armed
with meditation, a youth has but little to fear
from the devil; but if he neglects it, he runs
into battle without arms. How do you treat
your flowers? You refresh them with pure
water every day; and your soul, that beautiful
lily, shall she lack her dew?

Prayer is to the soul what water is to flowers;
deprive them of water, and the flowers wither.
Join good reading to prayer; choose the best
and most solid books, suited to your vocation.
Seek above all, those that lead to contempt of
the world, and esteem of eternal things. God,
by means of good books, often excites holy
thoughts, and nourishes them with good examples.

Converse often with your Spiritual Father,
and learn from him how to conquer the temptations with which the devil molests you: for
the devil will make the best use of the little
time that remains to him, to gain your soul.
If you speak openly and candidly of your temptations and difficulties, you will find great helps
for your guidance amid the perplexities which
disturb you. St. John Climachus fears the ruin
of him who embarks in this affair without a
pilot, but promises a happy passage to him,

who allows a skilful navigator to conduct him. If you have a good friend on whom you can rely, and who would not for the world oppose your good desires, converse with him on the happiness of serving God, and the dangers of the world, and you will find in his discourse food for your fervor.

You may also practise some penances and mortifications, like those used in the order you propose entering. Vocation is not a flower that grows among soft and tender plants, but like the rose, it buds and blooms among thorns. Luxury and pleasure make it droop in your heart, but mortification always gives it new vigor. Practise especially self-denial, modesty, and obedience, for these are common to all religious orders. Thus have many done, who aspired to a Religious life. Imitate them, for they were successful; and be confident, that having begun the good work, you will bring it to a happy conclusion.

CHAPTER VII.

SECTION 1. *How are we to resist those who attack the most perfect choice.*

E who wishes to live piously, says St. Paul, must suffer persecution from the wicked who wish to seduce him, and from the good who wish to prove his virtue. How will you speak to both of these? A young Roman desired to consecrate himself to God in religion, and his parents engaged a Religious to turn him from it. The Religious asked him, why he wished to leave the world? To save my soul, replied the youth. "But I have never heard," said the Religious, "that one must needs enter a convent to save his soul. All states lead to Heaven. Read the Bible; there you find that the heavenly spouse seeks her beloved *in the streets and in the broadways.* It is therefore very evident that one can find God and secure salvation in the highways of the world, as well as in the religious cloister." The youth remained for a while silent and perplexed. "Observe," said he at length, "that

208

He is *sought* there, but not *found*. I pity you
very much, Rev. Father, added the youth smil-
ing, for you have been greatly deceived in retiring into a monastery, when you could easily
have reached Heaven by the broad road of the
world."

Relatives and friends generally make the first
difficulties. They are impelled by a false love
which is even worse than hatred. They say
that inexperienced youths ought not to resolve
on so important a step, because they will open
their eyes when it may be too late, and will see
that they have left what they did not know;
and, consequently, will either give way to
despair or leave in disgrace the life of their own
choosing. Finally, what harm can there be in
reflecting long on so important a step? Did
not Jesus say: "Which of you having a mind
to build a tower doth not first sit down and
reckon the charges that are necessary, whether
he have wherewithal to finish it." So, having
to raise the tower of perfection, ought not the
youth weigh well his accounts in the first place,
and see whether he will be able to carry out his
undertakings or not? A choice which cannot
be changed ought to be maturely considered
during a great portion of life. A person reflects
well before changing his residence for a single
year. Ought he not, in the same way, reflect

18 *

for several years before he resolves to change residence, state of life, and society, for ever? Every day, and every year, furnish youths with new pleas for mature deliberation.

The reply is easy: Either these relatives deceive themselves, or the Council of Trent and other Councils were wrong, when they decided, that the age of sixteen is sufficient for making a profession, which is to be preceded by a year or more of probation. Who would dare to say, "I am right, the Councils are wrong?" The fear of leaving religion, through a want of sufficient reflection before entering, is void of foundation. Lancicius shows, in his work,—"De adolescentia recte traducenda"— that the greater part of those who do not persevere in religion are those who *enter at an advanced age;* when, according to you, they were more capable of making a good choice. Perseverance is not the fruit of our reflections, but a free gift of God. The more worthy we are of it, the more certain we are of obtaining it. But the more innocent one is, the more worthy he is; therefore, the question is this: *Will a few more years of intercourse with a sinful world find you more or less innocent than you are at present.* If less, then you are surer of perseverance by entering now than if you delay it. But, you will say, on the other hand, I must delay until I have corrected my evil habits. It would never do to enter religion because you *are* perfect, but because you *wish to be so.* Then you must ask yourself: *Can I correct my faults more easily in the world than in religion?*

It is true that Jesus has declared that a man must reflect before he builds the tower. I reply that he has also said, "Suffer little children to come unto me, and forbid them not;" and the person to whom he said, "If thou wilt be perfect, come, follow me," was very young.

Is it not the greatest of follies to seek no advice, to take no time for reflection before establishing yourself in the world — the beaten path to Hell — and, at the same time, to desire much advice, long deliberations and protracted delays before entering religion, the road to salvation by which multitudes of faithful souls have easily reached Heaven.

Relatives and friends say: "It is very true that when God calls, neither advice nor time for reflection is required; but the child is influenced by man, by his confessor, and, therefore, what confidence can be placed in his vocation. After four days novitiate he will return home, a disgrace to himself and his family."

This is not true reasoning; for it is one thing for a man to present good reasons for taking a

wise course, and another thing for him to be the
cause on account of which this course is taken.
If, when a person is induced by men to perform
a praiseworthy action, it follows that he does it
on account of men, the same objection must be
brought against the conversion of a sinner who
is moved to it by the words of a preacher; and
really there would be no such thing in the world
as divine faith, for faith comes by instruction:
fides ex auditu. Generally, a person can believe
nothing unless some man first tells him what he
is to believe, and the motives and proofs that
lead to it? What would you say of the proud
and impertinent servant who would do only
those things which he heard from his own
master's lips? Is God then the only master
whom you will not permit to send a man as
his ambassador? Is God alone not to be obeyed
unless he speaks in person? The Holy Ghost
generally withholds his inspiration until the
tongue of man opens an entrance: just as the
golden thread does not enter the cloth until
the needle has opened the way. You disap-
prove of these invitations, but St. Augustine
applauds them, and exhorts those who are in
the port, by the charity they owe their brethren
in danger of drowning in the sea, to help them
with good advice, to which they can cling as to
a plank, and be saved from shipwreck. If your

advice is prudent, St. Augustine's came from ignorance, or from a wish to deceive us. When youths of great hope leave the world, some people urge the advantage and the honor of their families and country. But either no evil consequences will result, or if any should, they ought to be endured in obedience to God. Have confidence in God, for he is a good Father, and will provide for the welfare of families and countries. It is a very estimable gain for a father or a country to give a servant to God who always returns an hundred-fold. Even suppose that you do experience some loss, does not God deserve that you should endure it in obedience to him? When a king calls any one to his court, he thinks only of obeying, and feels honored by the privilege of serving his prince. But you will say that the family and the country receive great glory and benefit from such a sacrifice. In reply let me ask, may you not expect the like advantages from the King of kings? O! my God, thou art indeed poor, if poverty and disgrace are the only rewards of those who are so liberal to thee. How many in religion have acquired for their families and their country a celebrity which will endure forever, whilst if they had remained in the world they would have been utterly forgotten.

SECTION 2. *Falsity of the accusations brought against the religious state.*

THERE are parents who say to their children: "Beware of dishonoring your family by muffling yourself in a habit and begging bread; rely upon it, in such a case I will never speak to you again." St. Augustine replies to these parents: "The profession of Christian humility is either vile or honorable. If honorable, why are you ashamed of yourself and your children? If vile, why do you respect it, even upon the altar?" Do you not reverence voluntary poverty in St. Francis of Assissium? Why then call it base? Do you not venerate religious humility in St. Aloysius? Why then regard it as a disgrace? Do you believe that these and many other saints would even be spoken of, if instead of humbling themselves before God they had bowed to the proud notions of worldlings? *Miratur*, says St. Jerome, *orbis pauperem quem divitem nesciebat.* The world admires the youth in poverty, whom it disregarded when rich. Among all the princes of Gonzaga, none has made the family so illustrious as St. Aloysius by his humiliations. When St. Louis, son of Charles II, king of Naples, and nephew to St. Louis, king of France, took the habit of St. Francis, some one said to him: What honor this garb receives from be worn by your royal person! On the contrary, replied he, weeping, I am honored by wearing it; and, poor as it is, I prefer it to all the royal mantles in the world. Henry II. having received from Pope Benedict VIII. a globe of gold as a token of imperial dignity, immediately presented it to the inmates of the monastery of Cluny, saying, "This symbol of the world belongs more to them than to me, since they nobly tread the world under foot by despising its vanities."

There are persons who declaim against religious orders; even employ the tongue of scandal in defaming them. When they cannot find a single fault in individuals, they defame the whole body of which they are members. If they know nothing bad, they leisurely create falsehoods, so as to disgust those who aspire to religious perfection. They say now, as they did in the time of St. Augustine, that Religious frequent courts too much, lay snares for their neighbor, mingle in affairs which their rules forbid; that they are dissolute, proud, quarrelsome, and relate other calumnies regarding them.

Ask these advocates of the world if they would advise you to remain in it in order to avoid these dangers. If they say " Yes," reply to them, that beforehand they must erase from the Gospel the many passages in which Jesus

Christ declares that the world, in all places, and all times, is filled with a thousand dangers But suppose what they say to be true of some order ; would you find as much wickedness in it as in the world ? If there should be a small number of unruly religious, ought we therefore accuse the whole body ? For two bad apples will you condemn the good, and cut the tree down ? Do not some physicians ruin the health of their·patients ? Some soldiers turn traitors ? Some worldlings become thieves and murderers ? Shall we therefore condemn all these states ? To judge of a state by exacting an infallible and unalterable rule, or a perfection incompatible with the liberty left to man, is only to deceive ourselves. All we can ask is, that the generality be good. A man once declaimed against the order of St. Augustine, because a youth had committed a fault. " Ah, well! " said the Saint, " I grant that there are some in the cloister, tainted with luxury, avarice, or pride ; but for that ought you to condemn all the religious ? How many adulterers among married persons ! swindlers among merchants ! and flatterers among courtiers ! However, you do not blame these states. Why act differently when you consider the religious state ? If one commits a fault, is he necessarily led on to it by all the others ? If a little cheat is found amongst the good grain, you do not conclude that all this is cheat. Then, to justify you in calling the good wicked, is it enough that some few wicked should be found amongst the good? But what do you require? Is it that monasteries be composed of persons confirmed in grace?"

There is not a single individual in the whole world who is confirmed in grace. All are weak, nay, very weak; and monasteries are composed of these weak creatures. But even suppose, then, all angels,—would it be astonishing that there should be a mixture of good and bad, as happened in Heaven? Let them be Apostles,— might there not be a Judas among them?

If you count the good and the bad, you will find the bad few, and their faults outweighed an hundred-fold by the labors and virtues of those who live regularly, as St. Chrysostom wisely observes. (L. 3.) The difference is, that whatever is bad is very soon spread abroad, is listened to with much attention, sought with great avidity, related with uncommon pleasure, and believed most readily; whilst whatever is good is often done in secret, and most men do not care to hear it, and believe it only with difficulty, because it stirs up remorse of conscience. You are well instructed in all the shameful falls of religious; but alas! you are ignorant

19

of the glorious victories of so many over temptations; the joy with which they endure contempt, poverty, sufferings and martyrdom; and their absolute command over all their passions. You know not their acts of humility, so painful to human nature,—nor their mortifications and penances, by which they strive to conquer their delicacy of body. The numberless examples of virtuous religious ought therefore to be more powerful in attracting you to a religious order than the rare falls of a few in removing you from a community noted for the faithful observance of the rule.

CHAPTER VIII.

SECTION 1. *Unhappy end of those who are deaf to the divine call.*

COULD relate many deplorable misfortunes which have befallen those who, through delay or negligence, have not obeyed the divine call, and after a long train of calamities, have ended their lives by a miserable death. I will give two or three of the most authentic. St. Antoninus relates the sad history of a young man of rare talents, who was called by God to the Order of St. Francis, and who resolved to enter it, but deferred his entrance from day to day. To increase the delay, he accepted the care of a parish. After a few days he was seized by a violent fever, and, that the world might know the cause of this punishment, he exclaimed in a frightful tone: "Ah! unhappy me; I have despised the voice of God: Alas! I am lost." They begged him to make his confession, but he refused, saying: "I am damned." They at first thought he was out of his senses, but in

the end saw that he was perfectly sensible. They spoke of the mercy of God, and urged him to promise obedience to his vocation, to kiss the crucifix and make a good confession. He replied: "I will not confess. I have seen Almighty God in wrath against me. I have heard from his mouth this irrevocable sentence: *'I have called thee, thou hast refused me: therefore, depart into hell.'*" After these words, the young man expired. Are you astonished at this? It is not at all strange, for St. Anselm says: "*How many have I known to promise and delay, who have been so surprised by death that they have neither been able to enjoy what induced them to delay, nor fulfil what they had promised!*" But here is another example which compels us to say: "*Thou art just, O, Lord! and thy judgment is equitable.*" At Turin, a young man gifted with fine qualities had resolved to leave the world, but he was turned from his resolution by a friend, or rather by an enemy whose affectionate letters promised such great enjoyments in the world that he gave up the thought of entering the house of God. The Spiritual Father of this deluded young man heard of the perfidy of his friend, and wrote to him to leave off his diabolical occupation, and if he desired the salvation of his companion, to advise him to fulfil his good resolution. "If you do not," says he, "you will experience what recently happened to a young man who left the service of God by the persuasion of another. He lived an abandoned life, was implicated in a robbery, and died on the gallows." All this was useless; the seducer persisted and the young man obeyed him. After some days he was arrested with a band of robbers, that had just assassinated some travellers. From his dungeon he wrote to the Priest, that his threat had been a prophecy, for he was then in irons as an assassin. To the great dishonor of his family he was at once condemned to death. Thus the word of the wise man was fulfilled : *"Because they have not consented to my counsel, but despised all my reproof, therefore they shall eat the fruit of their own way, and shall be filled with their own devices."*—(Prov. i. 30–'31.)

SECTION 2. *Those who flee from God's invitations soon receive their chastisement.*

WHAT I am about to relate has been published by Father Lancicius, an eye-witness. A boarder of the Roman College had received from nature great talents, was wealthy, and the nephew of a Patriarch. When old enough to choose a state of life, he asked to make a retreat, and began it with edifying sentiments. Having made a general confession with great care and

19*

delicacy of conscience, he asked if it was a sin
not to obey an inspiration to become a religious.
I understood what he was aiming at, says
Father Lancicius, and cautiously replied that
it was no sin; for the religious life is not commanded but only counselled. I added, however,
that it was very dangerous to reject such invitations; for many were damned, not because they
would not become religious, but for sins which
they would easily have avoided by being in the
cloister. The unhappy man, instead of believ-
ing me, wished to make the experiment. He
left Rome and went to the Academy of Macerata
to study law. His piety diminished, he neglected the sacraments, associated with young
libertines, spent his time in reading bad books,
and became enamored of a certain lady of the
city. One night, whilst going to her house,
he met a rival who gave him several mortal
stabs with a dagger. This misfortune happened
under the windows of the college. The poor
man cried out, " Confession! confession!" A
father heard him and ran in all haste, but alas!
too late! God grant that the life of the soul
was not lost with that of the body.

How terrible is the sentence passed by a God
infinitely just: *I called and you refused; you
have despised my counsel and neglected my
reprehensions. I also will laugh in your*

*destruction, and will mock when that shall
come to you which you feared.* When *sudden
calamity shall fall upon you, you shall call
upon me, and I will not hear because you have
not consented to my counsel.* (Prov. i. 24–30.)
This young man considered only the present,
to know if it was a sin not to embrace the
religious state. God, who foresaw his disaster,
gave him the means of saving himself, but he
would not use them To relate all the examples
of these rebellious souls who have died miserably,
would be a task as endless and as useless as
counting the dead to convince ourselves that we
must all die.

SECTION 3. *Misfortunes which have happened
to females who have despised their vocation.*

A VERY distinguished lady received many
favors from God, as long as she remained at
home passing her time in exercises of piety:
and as the grace of vocation was among these
favors, she resolved to consecrate her virginity
to God. But by degrees she left her retreat,
gave herself more liberty, and finally became
very fond of a young gentleman, who, in his
turn, conceived an affection for her. She forgot
her vocation, and thought only of hastening her
marriage. To celebrate the day with great
pomp, a numerous train followed her to the

house of her betrothed. * But in descending
from her carriage she slipped and fell so vio-
lently, that her neck was broken. Thus, she
expired before the door of the house which her
own will had chosen, instead of the cloister to
which God called her.

When the Countess Blanche retired to a
monastery, it was feared that she would abandon it on account of the four enemies which *
beset her: these were her noble birth, her
remarkable beauty, her youth, and the remembrance of her riches. Cardinal Peter Damian
wrote to the Countess, and, to encourage her to
persevere, related the tragical history of a great
princess who had disregarded her vocation. It
is as follows: Dominica of Gielva, a princess of
dazzling beauty, married a Doge of Venice, and
passed her life in pleasure and luxury, without
troubling herself with the service of God. The
purest dews of Heaven were collected for her
baths, food was nicely minced at table by servants to save her trouble, and her chamber was
filled with the most precious perfumes. You
can form no idea of the luxury that surrounded
her. Every day she spent several hours before
her mirror in painting herself, and would not
allow a single hair to be out of place. Divine
justice did not fail to overtake her. In a horrible sickness her flesh putrefied, and the smell

which came from her sores was so insupportable that she resembled carrion devoured by worms. Her maids and servants fled from her. A single attendant ventured from time to time to carry her some food in a silver bowl, but provided herself with perfumes, and retired quickly to avoid fainting. What a sight! to see this princess—lately so nicely perfumed, now nothing but corruption! the body that wore such costly attire, now nothing but ulcers! her who received the homage of all the great, now left to her servants! She to whose pleasure, nature, and art could not contribute enough, now lay eaten up by cancers, plunged in filth, a burden to herself, and insupportable to others. A little while ago she would not allow one to speak to her of death; now, death is the object of her most ardent desires. Let us finish this article by a sentence of St. Gregory: *"There are many who, unless they quit all, absolutely cannot be saved."* St. Theresa, after a horrible vision, often thought that she saw a bed of fire in hell which would have been hers, if she had not embraced the religious state. I wish that every one who feels himself called to forsake the world, would often ask himself: *" Who knows if this be not the only means left me for escaping temporal and eternal evils ?"*

CHAPTER IX.

SECTION 1. *Constancy is always crowned with success.*

 WILL now present you with a few examples of a heroic constancy in youths remarkable for a love of their vocation. Those who desire to embrace the religious state will thereby see how necessary it is to resist the wiles of the devil, without retreating a single step; and cowards, who fall from their vocation at the least difficulty, will have reason to blush.

Albert, who was born in Flanders of a family related to the King of France, was sent to the Court of Paris to be brought up with the King's children. His heart was taken up only with the heavenly court, and he conceived a lively desire of consecrating himself to God in the Order of St. Dominic. As soon as the Count, his father, discovered the first symptom of his inclination, although far advanced in years, he started post-haste for Paris with several rela-

tives and friends. On his arrival he set his
imagination to work, to devise schemes for
changing the mind of his only son and the sole
heir of his house. But in vain did he try, for
the love of God had steeled the child's heart
against carnal love. All his father's companions prayed him to relinquish his design,
but he resisted all their assaults, even their
jeers and their mockeries, which are often more
successful in overcoming a youth than threats
and torments. He perfectly followed the advice
of St. Augustine: "Oppose to these railleries a
holy resolution, and have a forehead of brass to
blunt the points of their tongues." Theodoric,
Albert's cousin, being much grieved at losing
him, employed every argument, resorted to
prayers and tears, to turn him from his resolution, and finally said: "Your mother is perhaps
dead or dying with grief caused by your design." There was a picture of the crucifixion
in the room, with Mary at the right of the
Cross, and St. John at the left. Albert gazed
at it for a moment, and pointing to it, said:
"Behold the Son of God who sees his own
mother and his beloved cousin, both so dear
to him and both pierced with a sword of grief,
and, notwithstanding his torment and theirs,
he remains on the Cross until death. Shall I
then dare to abandon the cross of a religious

life, only from motives of human love? No, I can never do it, not even if my dear mother were expiring before my eyes. Rather come with me, dear cousin, and embrace this holy cross; break through the dangerous snares which environ you; come and enjoy the liberty of the children of God." Albert's words sunk so deeply into Theodore's heart that he joined him, and they went to the monastery together, much to the surprise of all, because Theodore had, until then, been much addicted to vanity.

Lelius Ubaldini, a nephew of Cardinal Alexander de Medicis, resolved when very young to join the Order of bare-footed Carmelites. He mentioned it to his uncle, the cardinal, who, knowing the weakness of his constitution, told him that what he desired was above his strength, that he must reflect well, and, finally, all that seems inspired by the Holy Ghost ought not to be at once decided as coming from him. The resolute youth, wishing to try his strength, abstained from all comforts, slept on a plank, gave up the use of meat, fasted often, ate the food for which he had the greatest repugnance, and devoted his time to prayer and penance. After some time he was stronger than before, and his relatives therefore concluded, that austerity had given him new vigor, as was the case with the three young Babylonians who, after

long fasts, looked better than those who lived
on princely food; "their faces appeared fairer
and fatter than all the children that eat of the
king's meat." (Dan.) The uncle being convinced by this wonder, told the mother that he
could no longer in conscience hinder him from
going to the monastery. In the meantime Cle-
ment VII. died, and the uncle having to repair
to the conclave for the election, forbade Lelius
to execute his design before it was over. He
himself was elected; and when his holiness
received the token of respect from the general
of the Carmelites, he said: "Now I consent
to my nephew's entering your Order." When
the general withdrew, he met the nephew in the
street — with a great train of Knights — going
to kiss his uncle's feet, and told him the permission his uncle had just given. The youth
hesitated whether he should offer his homage
to his uncle, or give up this honor and leave
the world instantly. The love of God triumphed; he left the Knights, and, to their
astonishment, hastened to the monastery, and
put on the religious habit. In this robe of
penance he went to the Holy Father, and all
who saw him were bathed in tears. His uncle,
weeping, embraced him affectionately, and gave
him his own name, Alexander, saying: "Behold
the first genuine promotion I make; this is my

20

Cardinal of Jesus crucified. Persevere, my son,
in this holy state ; you will be happier than I
on earth and in heaven." What say you of a
heart so magnanimous? The sequel of his life
corresponded to its beginning, and he was num-
bered amongst the illustrious of his Order.

SECTION 2. *He who perseveres gains the victory.*

DESIDERIUS PALOTTA, nephew of the Cardinal
Archbishop of Cozenza, after a virtuous child-
hood, was called, at the age of fifteen, to the
religious state. He prepared for it by so many
exercises of piety that the Cardinal suspected
his design, and, to prevent its execution, removed him from Rome. But this change of
place made no change in the heart of Desiderius,
for he lived in retirement, frequented the sacraments, and by means of a secret correspondence
received advice as to the course he should pursue. He at length resolved to ask the Cardinal's consent, without which it would be difficult
to obtain the desire of his heart. He however
made the attempt, and accompanied it with the
most ardent prayers. The Cardinal had based
his greatest hopes upon the excellent mind
of his nephew, and the blow was, therefore,
severe. The resolution of Desiderius was known
at Court, and relatives, friends, and all the great
opposed it with their weighty influence. He

was not moved, but always rested upon the obligation of obeying a divine inspiration. The Cardinal took him back to Rome, and declared his difficulties to the Pope, begging him to interpose his authority. The next morning the young man unfolded the desire of his heart to the Vicar of Jesus Christ, and begged him — as the common Father of the faithful — to assist him in an affair so deeply affecting the interest of his soul. The uncle, being very much displeased with Desiderius, for speaking with the Pope, immediately stripped him of considerable gifts which he had bestowed upon him, and forbade his appearing in his presence. Desiderius, reduced to misfortune, without his usual pomp and retinue, repulsed by the lowest servants and exposed to those insults which young persons find so hard to bear, found the greatest consolation in saying, like St. Francis, *Pater noster, qui es in cœlis.*

The Pope, through regard for the Cardinal, wished the youth to continue his studies at Pisa. In the midst of licentiousness, he preserved his angelic morals, lived in holy retirement, and continued his practices of piety, such as penance and the frequentation of the sacraments. He was afterwards recalled home, where he had much to suffer for his vocation. To make himself worthy of the guidance of Heaven, he col-

lected the poor children, to whom he taught
catechism, established a confraternity of youths,
and did many other good works. He continually
sighed after the happy moment of his entrance
into the House of the Lord; but perceiving no
limit to the opposition he met with, he fled from
home, and, after travelling all night and the
half of the next day, arrived in Rome in the
evening. He immediately repaired to the feet
of His Holiness, and begged, that, since he was
unable, after so many proofs of his vocation, to
obtain permission to follow it, he would deign
to act in the affair as the Vicar of God on earth.
He prayed with so many entreaties and so much
earnestness, that the Pope immediately ordered,
that he should be received into the monastery.
He entered it overwhelmed with joy, and said,
that he was very thankful to his uncle, because
the severity of the battles made him enjoy the
victory the more.

SECTION 3. *Heroic courage of Females in the
affair of their vocation.*

THE young princess Frideburg, although promised in marriage to the King of France, resolved to give her life to God. The king had
assembled the chief men of the kingdom of
Metz, and finding the princess at church, he
invited her to the palace where he wished to

celebrate the nuptials. She fainted, and begged some days from the king that she might recover her strength. The king consenting, withdrew. When the time had elapsed, the princess went to the Church of St. Stephen with two attendants and two maids of honor. To the astonishment of those around her, she soon appeared in a religious habit, which she had secretly carried with her. She approached the sanctuary, prostrated herself, and, rising, stood close to the corner of the altar, where she pronounced the following prayer: "Blessed St. Stephen, who, first of all, shed your blood for Jesus Christ, I beg you to recommend to him the important affair which now engages my thoughts; so that by your intercession he may bend the heart of the king; and that I may not be stripped of the veil with which I am adorned through a love of virginity." The attendants hastened to inform the king of what had just occurred; who, as soon as he heard it, assembled the Bishops and Princes and asked their advice. The Archbishop of Arles replied, that he ought not to be the rival of Jesus Christ, and that he could not marry a virgin who sought heavenly nuptials. The king, filled with a fear of God, triumphed over the passion of love, and sent the robes and crown of the queen to the church. As he advanced towards her, she looked ten-

20 *

derly at the altar and exclaimed : " Alas ! my God, all is lost unless thou aid me quickly." Fear not, my child, said the king with goodness, I have come to preserve and crown your virginity. Your pious desires will this day be accomplished. The princess reclined her head upon the altar, saying : " Behold the handmaid of the Lord, be it done unto me according to thy word."

The king ordered the ladies to clothe the princess with the royal robes, gird her forehead with the diadem, and, without awaiting new solicitations, he said to her in a broken voice : " I intended that you should become my spouse, but it is just that I should yield you to our Lord Jesus Christ." Then, taking her right hand, he placed it on the altar to signify that he gave it to a more worthy spouse. All the courtiers were much affected. The king alone preserved his firmness, but, in leaving the church, he could not conceal the violent struggle within his breast between love and grief. His tears and sighs revealed the sentiments thus far hidden in his heart. He sent for the princess, seated her on the throne, loaded her with presents, and then permitted her to retire to the House of God. O ! inexpressible power of divine love ! One knows not which to admire most ; the constancy of a princess who prefers a veil to a royal diadem, or the piety of a king who prefers the service of God to his own tender affections.

I will mention a no less admirable example in the person of Sister Angelica of the Trinity, and the daughter of the celebrated Marshal Brissac. To a very distinguished birth she joined rare qualities of mind and heart, an exquisite beauty, and an amiability so perfect that many distinguished persons sought her hand. Their marks of attention only afflicted her, for she sighed to become the spouse of Jesus Christ. She employed all imaginable industry to succeed, begged the permission of her parents, addressed fervent prayers to the Saints, appeared badly clothed, feigned silliness, and in a word, no one has, perhaps, employed more means to gain hearts, than Angelica to estrange them. She disfigured herself by penances, washed her face in corrosive water and afterwards exposed it to the sun in order to change her complexion. She said, like St. Agnes, "Let the body perish which can be loved to the prejudice of God!" She spoke a little incoherently in company to make persons think her wanting in sense; and she did this so successfully that it seemed more from nature than virtue. With her the love of God, as St. Bernard says, was a holy folly. Finally she gained the victory and hastened to the monastery of the Carmelites with a joy far greater than that with which some young persons contract the most advantageous marriages.

Behold now, what youths of every age and sex can do with the help of grace when they are faithful to it. It remains for you to imitate them. If you are not frightened by the least noise, if you do not cast down your arms in the midst of the battle, if you stand firmly at your post, you will surely conquer. A high office in the army was vacant and belonged by right to a certain Marin, a soldier and good Christian. But his rivals tried to deprive him of it on account of the faith he professed. Being summoned before the tribunal, he appeared with composure, and was allowed three hours to decide whether he would leave the service of Jesus Christ or that of the tyrant. Teotecne, Bishop of Cæsarea; hearing of it, started for the court-room, and meeting Marin just as he was leaving the judges, led him to a church and advanced to the altar. He took the Gospel in one hand, and Marin's sword in the other, and said in a majestic tone: "You cannot possess these two objects at the same time. Choose the one or the other. Take either temporal glory with the sword, or eternal glory with the Gospel." Marin turned from the sword, seized the Gospel, kissed it, and pressed it to his heart, until the Bishop, who was much affected, said to him : "Keep well, my child, what you have chosen, and since you despise the honors of the present life, hope for those of life eternal."

I say the same to you. Keep well what you have chosen. You have received from God a signal blessing, a vocation to the standard of Jesus Christ. Take care lest you lose it by cowardice ; for then, the means you once had of reaching Heaven, now that you have neglected them, will only serve to cast you deeper into hell.

CHAPTER X.

SECTION 1. *Letters addressed by various holy Doctors to young men, to induce them to make a good choice.*

ST. FULGENTIUS, a nobleman of distinguished family, and whose talents and riches gave him every hope of success in the world, conceived a disgust for its vanities and a strong inclination to a religious life. See how he expresses his desires: "How unhappy are we who live in the world! Why do we undergo such labors without the hope of an eternal reward? What can the world give us which does not cost us far more than it is worth? If we wish to live in joy, why do we not reflect that the servants of God, whose conscience is tranquil and who fear only sin, taste a joy far purer than we? They are not burdened with secular affairs; they are not afraid of losing their riches, nor do they covet those of others. In the religious life they breathe the pure air of Heaven and find tranquillity of soul, security of conscience, union of wills, true friendship, happiness of heart, and all this amid persons entirely devoted to God. Those who are in this state of life invite us to join them, to enter the port and be sheltered from tempests. They exert themselves to help us in reaching this happy land where we will be free from the afflictions of the world, where the body is on earth and the soul in Heaven. Ah! let us hasten to embrace a state so estimable; let us not abuse the light Heaven has so profusely given us. Thus far we vied with our friends in gaining the honors of the world, let us now strive to imitate the humility of the servants of God." St. Fulgentius set out for the monastery to the great admiration of all Carthage, and was imitated by many persons distinguished by their birth, their talents, and their riches.

St. Augustine received an excellent poem from the young Licentius. He admired its elegance and conceived a desire of withdrawing so elevated a soul from the vanities of the world. In his reply to the young man, he said, amongst other things: " If your verses were irregular and little conformable to the rules of poetry, you would not rest until you had corrected them. Great God! your affections are not conformable to the law of God, you yourself are all in disorder and you do not perceive it, nor blush, nor seek to re-establish order in your heart! Will you do less for your soul than for a miserable verse? You have a tongue of gold, but a heart of iron. Oh! that I could persuade you to seek true peace of heart! Hear at least the incarnate wisdom, Jesus Christ, who addresses to you this affectionate invitation: "Come to me ye who are weary and heavily laden, and I will refresh you; take and carry my yoke, learn of me humility and meekness; then you will find peace of heart, for my yoke is easy and my burden light. Consider the example of Paulinus, who, from a great orator, became one of the poor of Jesus Christ. How long will you continue to be the sport of your ever-varying thoughts? Why will you listen to pleasures which reproach you whenever you enjoy them? Then turn your mind towards eternal things. I am sorry that I am unable to convert a young man endowed with talents so rare, which, if well employed, would contribute so greatly to the glory of God. Oh! how I long to offer him the sacrifice of such a soul! If you should find a golden chalice, you would quickly give it to a church. You have received from God a golden mind and you use it only to please the devil!"

St. Bernard endeavors to describe the happiness of those who sincerely give themselves to God and renounce the service of creatures. The God of consolation infuses the peace of Heaven into their hearts and makes them incomparably happier in poverty, than monarchs amid their

abundance. "Would to God," says he, in
writing to a young man, "that you would
attentively consider what are the objects which
deprive you of so great a blessing. Alas! you
would see that you renounce it for a vapor that
will vanish in a moment. If you are wise,
courageous, and clear-sighted, cease to seek
things, the possession of which will be your
misfortune. Is it not better to despise them
now with glory, than to lose them later with
grief? Is it not better to yield them now to
the love of Jesus, than a little later to the power
of death? I cannot, my dear Walter, restrain
my tears, when I reflect that you give your
youth and talents to sheer vanities. God will
demand of you an account of his blessings,
which he intended you should consecrate to his
glory, but which you devote to the service of a
world that gives nothing in return. A youth
delights in his birth, his health, his pleasing
exterior, his talents, and the society to which
he is admitted, but all the glory should be re-
ferred to God. If by usurpation you make his
gifts subserve your own pleasure and honor,
the Sovereign Judge will soon come to demand
the profit you may have gained from the talents
committed to your care. What will you reply
when he will reproach you with having received
your precious soul in vain? Will you point to

your studies, your projects, your labors, your riches, your honors? Rely not upon these, for death regards them not."

SECTION 2. *Other letters on the same subject.*

YOUNG Heliodorus having spent some time with St. Jerome, in Palestine, returned home to live in ease. The saint wrote to him as follows: "Listen, Heliodorus, to an edict issued by your Sovereign: ' He who is not for me is against me. He who is engaged in any thing except my service throws away his toil.' Remember the promise of fidelity you have so often repeated to Jesus Christ. Will you let the devil snatch the Saviour from your heart? Will you permit him to bear away the palm you could so easily have gained by fighting? What folly! When even your nearest relatives stretch themselves on the threshold of your house, pass boldly over their bodies. Even when all the world sheds torrents of tears, fly intrepidly to the standard of the cross. Who can blame you for leaving man for God, earth for Heaven? It will come, yes, that happy day will come, when you will be called to your country, when you will enter with the crown of triumph into the heavenly Jerusalem. Then you will beg the same blessing for your relatives, and for me who cheered you on to the combat. I am sensible how heavy are the chains that retain you. I too have a heart of flesh and human feelings, and have experienced the same difficulties that you now experience, but I have passed through them all. A sister begs, implores you, not to abandon her; an affectionate mother recalls the pains of child-birth, and the care she has bestowed upon your education; you are regarded as the only support of your family; but if you have a spark of love for God, or the least fear of hell, you will nobly despise all these obstacles. What! the enemy comes to destroy you, and you stop to consider the tears of your mother! Will you desert the heavenly band of soldiers, to hear the lamenta-tions of a father whom you are not even obliged to bury when God calls you? See how the Apostles left all! The Son of God hath not whereon to lay his head, and you wish for palaces? I speak with full knowledge of all these dangers. My poor bark, like so many others, struck the rocks, and I saw myself obliged to cast overboard all I possessed in order to save myself. Like an experienced sailor, tossed by the tempest, I cry to all whom I see exposed to danger: Be on your guard; in this gulf the Charybdis of pleasure opens to swallow you; there, Scylla allures you to pre-tended pleasures. Open, then, your eyes; do not be cruel to yourself; do not believe that you are safe because the sea is calm. The danger lies in its bosom; the enemy is in ambush under your feet. Hasten your flight; this tranquillity is the most terrible tempest you have ever seen.

"On the other hand, consider how safe one is when retired from the world, in this solitude abounding in those precious stones with which the city of God is built; in this hermitage separated from men, where one enjoys the sweet conversation of God! What are you doing in the world, my brother? you who are more noble than the world? Believe me; this desert is watered with the holy dews of Heaven; the less one seeks therein the satisfaction of the body, the more he finds that of the soul. Do you fear poverty? but Jesus Christ calls the poor 'Blessed.' Fatigue? but without it can a soldier gain his crown? The hardness of your bed? but see Jesus extended on the cross. Solitude? but direct your thoughts to Paradise where there is no weariness.

"The Apostle replies to every difficulty in the eighth chapter of Romans, where he tells us, that all we can suffer in this life is small when compared with the glory of Heaven. You cannot enjoy yourself both in this life and in the life to come. Take courage, then: your austerities will be rewarded by a happy eternity. The Divine Judge will be an object of terror to worldlings, but his poor disciples will behold him with extreme consolation."

A certain youth named Andrew having resolved to consecrate himself to God, was on the
point of giving up his resolution and plunging
into the tumult of the world. St. Gregory the
Great wrote to him in these terms:

" How deeply I am grieved to learn that you
aspire to the court; you whose happy dispositions gave me far different hopes! How
many have I known amid the turmoils of the
court to complain of having lost their peace of
heart! Then, reflect that you must soon give
an account to the Sovereign Judge. What will
it then avail you, to have been great at court
and dear to your emperor? Will you on that
account, be great in Heaven and dear to God?
Perhaps on that very account you will be neither
great nor dear. The fortune you expect at court
is very uncertain; that in the House of God is
perfectly sure. Earthly goods do not satisfy
the desires, they last only for a moment; but
those of infinite happiness are eternal. Can a
man of sense, a Christian, make such an exchange? If you desire riches, let them be eternal. If you fear misfortunes, let them be such
as never end. Would you have at the court all
you desire? What weariness in procuring the
favor of the prince! what fear of losing it! But
in the House of God a good life brings so much
consolation, that it may be compared to the joy

21 *

of Paradise. I speak to you thus, my child, because I love you dearly, and seeing you carried away by the tempest, I throw you a rope to draw you safe to the shore."

SECTION 3. *Comparison between those who labor for the world, and those who serve God.*

WE find in the letter of St. Eucherius to the noble Valerian, on " Contempt of the World," that the difference between the slaves of the world and the servants of God is this: the former have a cruel and inhuman master whose laws are barbarous, the latter, one who is all goodness and is continually occupied with the happiness of his vassals; the hearts of the former are filled with torments produced by the remorse which rends them, the latter enjoy a profound peace which the Holy Scriptures call a continual feast: the former can expect, as a reward for their labors, only a frightful punishment in eternity, the latter hope only for an immortal crown which the God of mercies prepares for them.

St. Cyprian wrote to Donatus to induce him to leave the world. These are the motives he presents: "Ascend with me, my dear Donatus, to the top of a mountain, where we can gaze together on the picture the world presents to our eyes. Behold how its highways are beset with assassins, how it is infested with armies

which contend to death under pretext of valor.
A private murder is a crime, a public duel
heroism. Cities are filled with imposture and
fraud. People run in crowds to obscene plays,
where, by foul jests and impure actions, they
praise vice and blame virtue; tender children
learn to do what they have so often heard of.
Custom persuades men that certain actions are
not criminal, public sentiment induces them to
crime, and, admiring the vicious, they seldom
fail to imitate them. The poison of lascivious-
ness enters by the eyes and ears and reaches
the heart; and he who came to the play with
an angelic mind, leaves it with one filled with
abominations. What ravages among souls!
what incentives to sensuality! But this is
only a little. If from the height of this mountain the eye could penetrate into the secret
recesses of families, we would see crimes so
great that barely to look at them would be to
commit a horrible sin. The greatest crimes
are committed in obscurity to cover the perpe-
trators from infamy. One condemns in public
what he himself does in secret. Fraud is called
address, and one is a great man only in pro-
portion to his wickedness. Let us glance at the
tribunals of justice. Let us see if we do not
find virtue, at least, in the ministers of the law.
Alas! here is still another refuge and another
mask for vice. Laws are disregarded, abuses

allowed, and crime stalks boldly through the
world. Innocence is driven forth defenceless,
and who will protect her? The advoca. ? he
seeks but to deceive. The judge? he sells his
conscience to him who will be guilty of the
greatest number of perjuries and calumnies.
The balance turns not beneath the weight of
reason, but under that of gold; property is taken
from one and given to another. Thus, it is a
glory to be guilty, a crime to be innocent.

"But perhaps you will say that I speak only
of the evils and say nothing of the good in the
world. Let us, therefore, enter palaces and
there contemplate the happy ones of the earth,
those who enjoy in abundance all that man can
desire of honors, authority, riches, and sensual
pleasure. Solomon, who was better provided
with all these pretended advantages than any
other human being, tells us that all is vanity;
either because the pleasure of the body is nothing when compared with that of the mind, or
because nothing remains in the evening of all
we have tasted during the day. These pleasures, moreover, carry with them a deadly
poison to the heart. See a courtier in the
highest offices of trust—with what servility
must he not labor, how basely must he not act,
what contempts and rebuffs must he not endure!
What watchings and labors are the share of the
ambitious, who are, moreover, continually agi-

tated by envy and hatred! What anxieties rend the heart of the merchant, who thinks only of gaining much and losing nothing! What is still more astonishing, in the midst of all his affliction, in his vessel exposed to shipwreck and so badly rigged, he is only a slave, and not the less abject because his chains are of his own choosing. But, at least, princes live in peace? Not at all: they fear others more than others fear them. Their greatness brings them only troubles, and, generally, the higher they are elevated, the more danger they are in of falling. Therefore, let him who seeks peace on earth depart from earth's uncertain goods, and retire into the harbor of a perfect life: let him raise his eyes towards Heaven whence he expects his consolation; and despise all else: let him rest all his hopes on God, desire only his favor, and fear only his displeasure."

Let us learn from St. Francis Xavier what is the happiness of a soul consecrated to God without reserve. He says:

" In reviewing the fruit of my poor labors, my heart is filled with so great a consolation, that I forget all I have to suffer, and shed tears of joy and consolation. Would to God that I could make the youths of the academies of Europe, who devote their talents to the acquisition of perishable goods, not only know, but also experience the contentment I experience in the midst of my labors. I am certain that great numbers of them would come to employ their talents and strength in saving souls. O God! only repose of those who seek thee, grant us such a disgust for creatures, that love may force us to come to thee. Render our hearts sensible of their past errors, that henceforth we may seek thee alone, be all thine, and live in the happy repose which thy faithful friends enjoy."

Now, dear reader, see what the desire of being useful to you has induced me to do. If any one thinks I am too fond of a religious life and too averse to the world, I beg him to examine if the fault is not on his side; if he is not too fond of the world and too averse to a religious life; for self-love loathes the good which is opposed to it, and delights in the evil that suits its inclination.

It would be a great misfortune if you are misled in the very important affair of the choice of a state of life. You would have to repent of it continually. Your regrets would be unmingled with consolation, and you would deserve so much the less pity, because, after having read these reflections, you could no longer plead ignorance, for your error would be but the result of your bad will.

SUBJECTS FOR REFLECTION.

God has given me this life to serve him: it is very short: if I lose it, he will not give me a moment longer. Oh! if a damned soul could obtain one moment!

I must soon die, leave my relatives, friends, riches, and pleasures, and appear alone before the judgment-seat of God: Oh! what a misfortune if I should there be placed among the reprobate!

What will be the joy of those who serve God faithfully in this life, and who say of the world: *Vanity of vanities and all is vanity, except to love God and serve him alone.*

What will remain of worldly pleasures? Remorse of conscience, God's wrath and eternal perdition. The body so much flattered will become first the food of worms and afterwards of eternal flames.

Regard the passion of Jesus Christ as an abyss of love, a treasure of infinite goodness. This is the school in which so many saints have learned to suffer and conquer. They were weak like you: why not imitate them?

There is no pure joy except in the service of God and in purity of conscience.

During life often descend into hell, to avoid being condemned to it after death. Would you wish to spend forty years of your life in a dungeon? Will you, then, be so foolish as to expose yourself to eternal fire, rather than employ your time well in this life?

What will it profit a man to gain the whole

world if his soul suffer for all eternity? What will he give in exchange for his soul?

Oh! foolish man! this night your soul may be called, and of what avail will all these riches be?

EXAMINE, 1st, What is the end of the state you desire.

　　"　　2d, What means you will have of living well therein,

　　"　　3d, What occasions of sin you will be exposed to.

　　"　　4th, In what you will imitate Jesus Christ therein.

　　"　　5th, What good works you will do therein.

　　"　　6th, What are your talents and strength of body.

　　"　　7th, In what you may be useful to your neighbor.

Be assured that nobody needs your services. Magistrates, officials, soldiers, &c., &c., will always be found without you. Candidates are not wanting. God takes care to provide the Church with Priests without your help. The religious have their particular state for themselves: your presence or absence will change nothing in it. If you die now, the world will go on the same as if you were living. There are indeed some useful men, but none are indispensable. Nobody has need of you, but you have need of knowing the will of God and of performing it. (Fenelon.)

www.ingramcontent.com/pod-product-compliance
Lightning Source LLC
Chambersburg PA
CBHW030807020726
47499CB00006B/1802